REIGNBOW

DIVISION OF REIGNBOW MARKETING INC.
1745 N. Ashbrook Circle
Mesa, Arizona 85203

Published by arrangement with
Reignbow Marketing Inc.

First Reignbow Printing October 1993

Printed in the U.S.A.

Author wishes to thank Monti Lawerence of Lawerence Semiconductors, Alan Hald of MicroAge Inc., Dianne Moore of Cereus Letter Processing, Thomas Stricker for the excellent cover art, West Bowes of Biotech West Germany, Michael Clifford of Hope Hospitals, Blain Andrews Graphics, Ray Buse Printing, Virginia at TBN, Kristy York, Ricky Timas, Jay Walkney, Larry and Barbara Stewart, East Chop Tennis Club and Stanford University Alumni Association.

CHAPTER ONE

THE SWARM

Underneath the decaying temple wall of the old Shou Lin Monastery, a teaming mass of small ones swarmed over one another creating a continuous tumult. They had dwelt in darkness for years and were anxious to escape their pit to spew out their deadly poison in the hearts of men.

On top of them and totally oblivious to their presence, the Chinese workers were clearing away portions of the rubble to make room for another Tannersly Factory. Had they known what they were about to let loose, they would have dropped their picks and shovels, abandoned the backhoes, cement mixers, pallets, and run for the polluted Pearl River.

"Don't give anyone time off today for lunch," Wedge shouted to his supervisor, Chen Lieu. "We're still running behind."

Wedge was short and stocky. He probably had a Napoleon complex, having always been shorter than his schoolmates and most of his girlfriends—that was, up until he found shorter Chinese girls to go out with. He was a third generation English Colonel who had no tolerance for lazy workers. Although labor was plenteous and cheap, he expected them to work until their hands were literally bleeding.

Chen Lieu took a different view of human life. Many of the workers had been converted to the ways of the Mighty One through the constant barrage of radio programs and literature, some of which were dropped through planes. Chen Lieu had been a follower of the Mighty One for years. He had grown to love his fellow countrymen and tolerated the cruelty of Wedge with divinely-inspired patience.

He heard one of his workers, Safrong Hochow, screaming hysterically and rushed over to see what the problem was, expecting the worse. A crowd of workers had pressed in around her and were choking off her oxygen.

"Move aside," Wedge commanded, elbowing his way through. He looked at her lying on the ground. "Everyone get back to work."

Chen bent down beside Safrong and lifted her head, addressing her in Cantonese. "What seems to be the problem?"

She responded in a choked voice, "While I was removing that rock with my pick, I glanced down. A creature came out of the hole. He was only three inches tall and was covered with a grotesque red fur and had ears that looked like an elephant. He cursed at me and disappeared."

She didn't realize that she had set the first of the small ones free from over 50 years of bondage.

Lubato, the hideous Imp, had been banished by the legendary Watchman Nee after Nee had resigned from the Shou Lin order embracing the Western Faith of Christianity. For as long as Lubato could remember, he lived in the temple in the small statues of dragons, snakes, and frogs. He and the other small ones had given the lifeless images power, and they roamed the countryside answering their suppliants' petitions just so long as the petitions were accompanied by gifts of flowers, coins, trinkets, and sometimes the suppliants' own body parts. Lubato had detested being in the swarming mass and had developed his sense of hearing so that he was in a position to escape should the opportunity arrive. He would listen year after year to the many tourists that visited the temple ruins and knew that someday he would again be free.

He was as surprised to see Safrong as she was to see him. When her pick came down he grabbed it. Because he had been totally blind for so long, he never realized that in the light his body had materialized again. The minute he saw her reaction, he simply shifted dimensions and became invisible to her, seeking to be unseen by man.

Wedge Harwood, Vice-President of Tannersly, was concerned only with the bottom line. He still thought of the Chinese the same way the American railroad builders in the

1800s thought of them—cheap, expendable labor. He knew that when one faltered or walked off the job, there were a thousand more waiting to work for the same low wages. He was glad to be out of Hong Kong with the trade unions, workers' rights, and thousands of other regulations that went with being a British Crown Colony. He was happy to be on the mainland where everything could be bought. He knew the plant in China would not have to have adequate rest rooms, dining facilities, or even more than a token health clinic for the workers. He knew they could dump their untreated sewage directly into the nearby river and not worry about any public liability lawsuits for cancer or birth defects. It was perfect for a company that sought to exploit and profit while spending as little as possible.

Seeing the workers stop and gather around Safrong, set him on edge. He had promised himself the foundation would be ready for the pouring of concrete in less than two days and he was determined that nothing would stop him.

"She looks like she's seen a ghost! What's wrong with her? Can't you tell everyone to get back to work?" he shouted to Chen Lieu.

"I have. She claims a small demon grabbed her pick and cursed at her."

"Well, tell her to go home early. Tell her she'll even be paid for the whole day, but have everyone else get back to work." Wedge Harwood grasped his side and wondered what the pain was. He scratched at it uncomfortably as he gestured with his hands. "Everybody back to work."

Lubato had found his host. He had seen the gaping hole in the side of Wedge Harwood and decided to take up habitation to get as far away as possible from the underground hellhole. He had never inhabited a human before; his only habitations had been lifeless idols. The hole in Wedge's side was not a physical one. It was in his spirit and was caused by a deep hatred and bitterness of the Chinese. Years of brashness, cruelty, abuse, and greed had left an opening in his spirit that Lubato was drawn to. He didn't want to take any chances with being bound and cast again beneath the temple floor.

As Safrong was carried away, the opening in the foundation began to crawl with activity. Those close to Lubato crawled out into the fresh air and sunlight. By the thousands they began to roam about the old temple grounds searching for new habitations.

* * * * *

That night when Wedge slept, he dreamed of things that he had never imagined before. His life seemed to spiral down as if in a giant vortex. He tried to open his mouth to cry out, but he found himself unable to speak. A feeling of unbelievable panic came over him and his silent cry of terror went out unheard. The blackness he descended into was colder than a frosty Arctic wind. The cold was not something that caused him to shiver, but rather, something that caused him to reflect on his life and ask himself, "Why is this happening to me?"

His live-in Chinese girlfriend, Grace Won, was usually a very heavy sleeper. She heard the moaning and woke up, looking over. In the glimmer of moonlight that showed through their rice paper window shading, she saw his face growing more and more grotesque. She grabbed him by his shoulder and shook him until he awoke.

"Wedge, Wedge," she said as she leaned over him, "wake up! You've been having a nightmare."

Wedge came back as if from the dead. It took him several moments to even realize who and where he was.

"What . . ." he rubbed the sleep out of his eyes. "Who . . . Grace? You woke me up. I was going down this long, black tunnel. There was no end . . ."

Grace leaned over and touched his hands. "Your hands—you feel like you're freezing. You sure you're okay?"

"I don't know."

Grace spooned in behind him to keep him warm. Lubato smiled with glee. It was the first time he'd ever been inside a creature so intelligent, and yet he had been able to make it see his thoughts, dream his dreams. None of it had really been a dream. Eons ago, along with many others, Lubato had fought against the Mighty One and had found himself on the losing side. He had performed valiantly, never realizing that the one who promised him victory was the Father of All Lies; there was no way out by the time he realized he had been duped. The void that he found himself in ended when he, along with thousands, of the other small ones, had been sent to China. Because of the smallness of their stature, they hid in the carved ivory and jade and had inadvertently moved some carved ivory pieces. They found it delighted the humans to see them move the carvings. Eventually, many of the small ones took residence inside the statues, granting small wishes of their devotees. They all enjoyed enslaving the humans by soliciting worship and homage. At night, when the humans would sleep, they would all leave their hosts and fly about through the countryside bringing pestilence, blight, and as much sickness and havoc as they could create. It wasn't long before there were temples and large statues built and the ranking fallen ones began taking dominion and control over entire areas. Lubato, along with the small ones who inhabited the old Shou Lin Monastery, quickly found their range of influence limited by Maduke, who demanded more. Out of rebellion to Marduke, the reigning principality of the area, they began to teach the Shou Lin monks lessons they had learned before the throne of the Might One. Through Lubato's instructions, the monks learned acts of benevolence, charity, love, kindness, patience, and became a false hope for the millions whose lives were ruled over by the tyrannical emperors under Marduke's influence. Several of the Shou Lins had seen the small ones and had talked with them personally.

Lubato had a long-term relationships with a devotee, Fushong Londee, who lived from 1895 until the Japanese invaded in 1938. Fushong had made many inquiries of Lubato and had finally learned that Lubato was severed permanently from the grace and love of the Mighty One. Lubato was so warmed by the attention and kindness shown to him by Fushong, that against every grain of his being he had finally confided to Fushong that his purpose in life was to deceive and trick the masses into missing the Salvation of the Mighty One and spend their eternity in the Lake of Fire.

Lubato had worried that after learning his true purpose, Fushong would have no more time to spend with him. Instead of finding hatred, he only saw the tears that Fushong shed when he realized that nothing would ever restore Lubato to fellowship with the Mighty One. Fushong changed his name to Watchman Nee and began the work of converting the other monks and then his countrymen, utilizing a book that he had found entitled *HOLY SCRIPTURES.* His work had not gone unnoticed by the government, and the last time Lubato had heard about him was when Fushong was sentenced to prison where his hands and feet had been cut off. Lubato and his minions had then been bound and confined to the pits of darkness for over 50 years and were quite anxious to stir up whatever trouble they could.

Safrong Hochow had attended the meeting of her small prayer gathering and told them of the creation she had seen by the old temple site. They all seemed concerned, but none of them took the matter with a degree of seriousness. Safrong knew the situation was much more serious and wondered why none of the followers were interested in praying about it. After finishing a short time of fellowship and a reading of the scriptures, she left for her small dwelling. The sky overhead, with the full moon lighting her way, cast an ominous shadow on the path. She felt an involuntary shiver pass through her loose silk-flowered garment and raced along hurriedly in her sandals. Her husband, Tulee Hochow, did not like her spending time with the fellowship, but he could not argue with the happiness and peace that it brought to her. He was content to watch slapstick entertainment on their small television set and drink their rice wine. The government had allotted them one child, and they had chosen to wait until they were both more settled with their jobs before they had their child. She was determined that even if her husband was not a follower, her child would definitely be.

The next day the workers came at 6:00 a.m. to remove some of the remaining old stones and smooth the dirt for the pouring of the new foundation. The small ones swarmed about unnoticed. Whenever they could during the course of the day, they would roll a stone down on someone's foot or cause a shovel to hit someone else. Nearly 70 people complained to Chen Lieu of injuries. Most were small except for Muchong Delwee, who had seen his thumb severed when struck with a shovel. They had put him in the back of the excavation truck and dropped him off at the infirmary where he had waited the entire day for his thumb to be reattached. It had been too long. Gangrene had set in and when the doctor had finally gotten to him, the thumb was a useless lump of flesh. Safrong wondered why so many were being hurt, but she did not notice the thousands of grotesque creatures that were causing constant mayhem.

"Are you still seeing little funny men?" Chen Lieu asked Safrong as she stepped up for her lunch of egg rolls and won ton soup.

Safrong was puzzled by the direct word spoken to her. "No, I'm not seeing any today, but isn't it odd how many accidents there have been. Until today we've had hardly any." She walked off knowing that she had given Chen Lieu something to worry about.

To save money, the Tannersly Company had decided to keep the outside wall of the temple intact and use it as the main production office. An entire corrugated steel warehouse was added on to the original temple. The building would easily house up to 10,000 workers. Already hundreds were showing up every day requesting jobs. With over two billion people in residence, the Pearl River area of China had no problem with labor shortages.

Wedge Harwood was under a strict deadline that allowed no slip-ups. The founder's granddaughter, Mia Tannersly, had decided to market a computerized toy for children called "The Imps." She had purchased much of the technology in Silicon Valley adjacent to where she had gone to college. She was intent on introducing the new line of toys before any of her competitors could get the jump on her. Wedge had three weeks to get the building ready and start bringing in the injection machines.

The phone rang.

"Wedge Harwood here," he answered, out of breath from running to catch the phone.

"Wedge, it's Mia. How's everything coming along?"

"We're a little behind schedule. One of the workers claimed to have seen a creature during the excavation. We missed most of yesterday afternoon. Today we've had several pretty bad accidents."

Mia was concerned that delay meant a loss of money. "Like what?" she asked impatiently.

"One worker lost his thumb, there were various puncture wounds, people were hit by flying rocks, all minor stuff, but a lot of it." Wedge tried to downplay the seriousness of the situation.

"Damn it, Wedge, we've got to get the thing done. We've got all the chips in and the molding machine just arrived crated from Arizona. Top notch plastic injection. We can do at least 10 thousand pieces a day." Mia bit her lip in anger and wiped away the flowing blood, surprising herself with her own fury.

"Miss Tannersly, you pay me well and I appreciate it. But I'm not a miracle worker. We are using unskilled labor. Look, I'll put on a third shift and we'll work all night if that'll make you happy, but you've got to send another factory manager. Nobody can work round the clock."

"I'll do better than that. I'll come over by helicopter tonight myself. Do you have any decent quarters?"

"No, not for rent, but I'll let Grace know you're coming. You can stay in the houseboat with us. We've got plenty of room. Look, we're putting up one of the walls now. I've got to go."

Wedge hung up the phone and hurried out to the yard where the west wall was being erected. What could have easily been done with big cranes and forklifts was, instead, being done with handmade rigged equipment and thousands of cheap laborers. Although Wedge hated the Chinese, he admired their ingenuity. After all, what other race had built anything that was visible from outer space? He had climbed the great wall of China and was truly impressed. He didn't even consider Grace to be Chinese. When he had taken the time to really get to know individuals, he had grown to love them. Today he was troubled. There was something eating away inside of him and he couldn't figure out what it was. Several of the women in their last months of pregnancy were struggling to lift the west wall. He had gone up and insulted them, calling them lazy and worthless. One had walked away in tears. The others just looked shamefaced down at the ground. He didn't know what was wrong—why he had become so cruel.

CHAPTER TWO

WAY BACK WHEN

Brian Phillips had been an outcast from nearly the very day he was born. His father, acting Dean of MIT, and mother, Brenda Holloway, nuclear physicist, were both members of Mensa. They both had charted IQs well over the 150 mark and had expected wonderful things from Brian. Even while in the womb, Brian was deluged with quantum physics and probabilities as his parents discussed their work each night over dinner. He was to be an exceptional child. They had wanted a boy, having already aborted two female fetuses that Brenda had carried before him. Had his sex not been male, he would have been dismembered as well.

In his nursery he had received a full diet of Wagner, Schuman, Beethoven, and his favorite, Grieg. He was musically apt at age three, and even though his feet could not reach the pedals on the piano, he could pick out the main themes to over 30 symphonies, much to the delight of the MIT faculty his parents loved to entertain.

"Brian, the Jacobs want to hear something by Granadas," his mom begged. "Brian, please?"

Brian put down his favorite talking Mickey Mouse and climbed on the bench of the family's old Mason and Hamlin 7 ft. grand. He began to play one of Granadas' Spanish melodies, turning around to relish in the praises of the adults. He knew when he was done they would give him a carrot stick and leave him alone to play with Mickey, Minnie, Pluto, and Goofy.

None of the kids in the neighborhood were deemed really suitable playmates for Brian. He was kept pretty much in seclusion. In the Boston suburb of Bunker Hill, he would look out of the windows at the children playing in the snow or on their bikes, wishing he could join in with them.

At the age four, his father bought him his first computer. It took him no time to begin understanding it. It soon replaced Mickey as his best friend. Within six months he was designing his own games and had even begun to take it apart to study it. His parents couldn't have been more pleased.

"John," Brenda said as her husband threw his coat down on their Victorian mohair-covered living room couch, "I think little Brian is going to need another computer."

"What?" John asked in amazement. "I thought we'd agreed he's not to take this one apart."

Just then Brian came down the stairs.

"Hi Dad." He ran up and gave his dad a big hug and kiss. "I couldn't get Charlie to respond and I took him apart to fix him, but when I put him back together, he sparked and blew up. I'm sorry."

John Phillips took one look at his son's innocent eyes and decided not to punish him. "Son, you just can't take everything apart." He took him by the hand and they walked up toward Brian's study. "But let's see if we can fix it. You've got to understand, son, these computers like Charlie are pretty expensive."

Most of the computers that Brian had were models given to MIT by various companies hoping to hook the students on their particular brands. They were always replacing them with new models and as John Phillips was acting President of the university, no one was opposed to him taking them out of the university storage. He made sure to pay the minimum for them, but since Brian had experimented with them since age four, he had already gone through over 30 different computer models. Brian was constantly redesigning the machines to make them more efficient. However, the main problem was, they were not designed with adequate power supplies. The latest computer that John had brought home was a forerunner in liquid memory and its functions were extremely rapid. At age 10, Brian had asked for permission to attend the computer classes at MIT and was regarded as an oddity in a college famous for its oddities and child prodigies. It wasn't long before the other students were seeking him out for help with their designs. They were baffled by the amount of knowledge he had.

John looked at the disassembled computer on Brian's desk. Again, it was the voltage supply. The fluctuation in commercially available power was the nemesis of every great computer programmer. Hundreds of hours of work were washed away by ebbs and surges from overloads in the city's voltage supplies. Surge protectors were not designed to really contain the low or high voltage surges, and in redesigning, Brian had so fine tuned his liquid memory machine that the slightest variation had caused a major malfunction and scorching of several of the main circuits.

"What do you think, Dad? I had it doing 1.5 megabytes. It was really awesome. We must have had a lot of power demand and they must have added on another generator."

John looked at the rapture in his son's face. He had long ago fought off the guilt of having kept Brian away from so many people his own age. He knew special people deserved special treatment. He didn't want Brian treated as he had been treated, dubbing him the school's "brain." He found himself victimized by the choice high school athletes and jock gangs who wanted term papers, math answers, etc. until they had literally frightened him into oblivion. Brian routinely made 10 copies of his homework and just handed them out before school everyday. John had tried to protect Brian from peer pressure, but knew that outside of his computer, Charlie, Brian had no life. He decided to make some changes and rented a vacation house for the summer on Martha's Vineyard. The summer took on more importance for Brian's social development because it was the only time Brian integrated with other children. The swim club and tennis club allowed Brian his few contacts with the outside world. At first his parents attempted to guard those contacts, but eventually they allowed Brian to come and go on his bicycle and explore the many paths and beaches the island had to offer.

"Yes," John thought, "my son has had a great upbringing. He's going to change his world."

One summer, before they were leaving for the vineyard, Brian's dad took him aside and said, "Tell you what, son. How'd you like to have your own small utility plant? I've been discussing with your mother the problems of these power surges and ebbs and we've decided to install our own miniature power plant right here in the yard. We've got some large utility batteries from our solar experimentations and all we basically need is a windmill. As long as we can get it by city hall, we're in business!"

"Does that mean I can regulate my own power supply?" Brian asked excitedly.

"Yes, to any voltage and ohm level you want."

"Dad," Brian's face beamed with happiness, "that's great."

"Now hold on, son. Until then, no experiments please. That's ten thousand dollars right there. Your mom and I make a pretty good living, but Uncle Sam is going to start wondering why we have so many deductions for computers. So for crying out loud, please just wait."

"How long?" Brian inquired.

"I'm hiring an attorney, Saul Rothstein, to get the variance. A few people at city hall owe him favors. He thinks he'll be able to run it through this summer while we're on the vineyard. It'll only take a week or two to get the windmill up. It'll be great as long as the neighbors don't complain."

"Do you think they will?"

"No, the Andersons are too old to care and the Todds never even got a permit for their new garage. I don't think they'll object. Still, we have to go through the proper channels."

True to his word, John's promises came true. When they were back only two weeks from a fun summer at the vineyard where he learned to set lobster traps and sail a small sunfish, the windmill construction began.

The whole house was wired to it, effectively removing the family from any further utility bills. The cost would have been staggering to the average family, but one of the MIT students was in charge of the large windmill operation in Palm Springs, California and had arranged to have a scaled-down model that was originally used as a prototype sent to Phillips. It had been in storage for years.

Brian was out in the yard everyday watching the crew put up the windmill and hook up the batteries. He understood better than all of them just how it worked and even made some small changes which surprised Scotty Johnson.

"You like me to what?" Scotty asked, surprised to find the youngster so well versed in electrical terminology.

"Instead of hooking all the batteries in sequence, set them in different groupings. That way when you off line, the charge-back you get will be reduced."

"How did you figure that out?" Scotty asked inquisitively.

Brian was happy to show him his computations and explain them in fuller detail. Scotty knew, armed with the information Brian had provided him, the main problems of the Southern California windmill power field could be solved. He was surprised at the simplicity of the solution. As the wind died down, the electricity that had been generated sometimes caused a burnout in the coils, which resulted in massive and expensive shutdowns and repairs as motor after motor had to be rewound. The fields for resistance were such that unless an ample amount of electricity was generated for storage, it would simply remain in the copper coils. Taking the batteries out of sequence lessened the resistance field making everything at least three to five percent more efficient.

That fall Brian began to think about his future. Lobsters fascinated him. His parents loved wildlife and had taken him to the state's lobster hatchery in Wood's Hole. Brian was fascinated with the way lobsters regenerated their own body parts. He was captivated by their movement and began to create on-screen programs in three-dimension that could move. Just the movement of a human thumb required a massive amount of information. Although robots were used to spray cars and to do mass assembly, they were still too primitive to handle an egg the way human hands could handle it.

He secured various materials from former MIT graduates who headed research labs throughout the country. He knew by further developing his fuzzy logic and neural networking, he could develop a chip that would enable a three-dimensional figure equipped with the right sensors to be virtually alive. It could compute distance parameters and with enough megabytes, could nearly duplicate the human brain—true artificial intelligence.

He set about creating his own roboticized lobster. One of the lobsters died in his backyard right before molting. Brian epoxied and wired the lobster's shell and installed laser sensors in the head, using robotic armatures he designed on the claws and pincers. In the tail section he stored the microprocessor and lithium battery.

Hour after hour he sat up in his home laboratory working on Louie the Lobster as he had affectionately dubbed him. He made his parents promise not to bother him while he was working and not to even ask about his project. He had read in *Popular Science* about a contest for young inventors offering a $2,500 first prize. He was intent on winning it but even more intent on bringing Louie to life.

Through MIT alumnus David Walton at Johannes Research in South Africa, he had finally secured a silicon-based material that was nearly as touch sensitive as the human skin, able to detect differences between real and artificial silks. He had cut up parts of the material, wired it to the sensors and into the circuit board, and began performing tests. He programmed the lobster to walk at different speeds across different fabrics which he took from his mom's old dresses. He cut them up and hot glued them on a homemade runway where he conducted performance tests with Louie.

He knew for a robot to be successfully used in society, it would have to be able to respond as quickly as any human or animal brain to outside stimuli. He knew that the five senses of touch, smell, sight, taste, and hearing all worked differently for different creatures. He was aware that the sense of smell was keenest for a wolf who could smell a potential mate up to 15 miles away, and he knew a male dog could smell a female in heat up to a mile away. He knew the sense of sight was especially keen with eagles who could sight their prey from great altitudes. He studied a book by a zoologist, developed his own formula to replicate an eagle's sense of vision, and began to program his microprocessor to control two separate laser scanners. It was by and far the most difficult set of experiments he had ever devoted himself to and he found himself becoming an excellent amateur veterinarian. As the year went by, he knew that his experiment was too revolutionary to enter into a contest, so he abandoned his plan of entering the contest and concentrated instead on perfecting Louie. He began to understand why creatures were designed with two eyes instead of one and discovered how depth perception was triangulated mathematically. The program he designed allowed for the slight differences in perception between his two laser scanners that he had mounted on Louie's head. It was a brilliant creation that could accurately calculate distance information almost instantaneously at unbelievable distances.

After he programmed in the average size of car head lamps, he found that Louie could predict the distance and speed of travel of oncoming traffic. Several times a week he snuck out with Louie and his lap computer and they tracked cars and trucks from the overhead walkway on the Beacon Street Expressway.

The school year passed and his parents got more and more worried about his participation. Brian merely went through the motions, constantly daydreaming about new experiments that he would be performing with Louie. The teachers never spotted even the slightest errors in any of his classes. He excelled in biology, math, geography, and art, and was physically fit enough to master all the phases of P.E. except the square dancing, which he detested. On his birthday his parents wanted to throw him a party, but when they were going over the invitations, they realized that they really didn't know any of his junior high friends. They weren't going to make an issue out of the importance of him making friends and they decided it was his choice.

What they didn't know was that Brian had a best friend: Louie. He was convinced Louie was the only real friend he would ever need. He had purchased various voice chips from AT&T and began to work on the neural networking, teaching Louie to respond to various commands and greetings.

Everyday when he came home and entered his lab, upon spotting him with his sensors, Louie would say, "Hello Brian, glad to see you back. Did you have a good day at school?"

"Hi Louie, yeah, it was great. How was your day?"

"I've just been watching out the window. There is a family of blue jays building a nest outside. It is fascinating to watch them flying back and forth with twigs."

"Any eggs yet?" Brian asked.

"No, not yet," Louie responded. "But I guess they wouldn't begin building a nest unless they had some on the way, would they?"

"No, you're certainly right, Louie," Brian interjected. "Say, I'm going down to the kitchen to get something to eat. Can I get you anything?"

"No thanks," Louie said. "I don't have much of a stomach for food anymore. Hurry back, though, I've been waiting for you all day."

Even though Brian had programmed hundreds of expressions, entire encyclopedias, and thousands upon thousands of bits of information, he began to think of Louie as a real person.

"Brian," his mom stated, "I didn't hear you get home."

"I came in the back. We got any good snacks?" Brian asked, opening the refrigerator.

"You can have an apple or some cheese and crackers. Please, no sweets. They'll spoil your dinner," his mom said. "Oh, by the way, your dad's bringing over a big shot from Cincinnati Milacron. He told him a little about your robot."

"Mom, it's not even finished yet. Louie would get embarrassed if I showed him off before he was even finished."

"Brian, Louie is you. It's your invention. I know you have a wonderful time working with it, but it's not real—not in the sense of the word that we are real. I wish I could make you see that."

As Brian stood munching on the apple, he looked at his mom. "Mom, don't you think somehow I could make Louie real?"

"Only God creates life, son. All we can do with our best effort is mimic His creation. Louie will never be real. Louie has no soul. No discernment between Good and Evil, right and wrong."

"Can't he be taught those things, Mom? Like you taught me not to lie or steal or cheat."

"He can be taught rules and regulations, but never the moral difference between right and wrong. No matter how many rules he knows how to obey, how many phrases and questions he can respond to, he'll always be a robot."

Brian was clearly disappointed, and his mom looked over and put down her cutting knife to give her son a hug and to comfort him.

"Someday God will bring you someone who loves you of their own free will. I know it's hard on you being the smartest one in the class, being an outcast, but once you're older, you'll meet others who'll like you for who you are. Just like your father and I met. Someone out there will love you."

"Mom," Brian asked, "who is God? How come only He can make life?"

"God is different for every person, Brian. For some people He is a best friend, someone they talk to everyday. For others he's like an omnipotent creator who made the earth and went on a holiday."

"How do you believe, Mom? What do you think about God?"

"I think He's probably really good and also really sad. Maybe He's sad that He ever made us and we cause so much pain for each other. He's someone I hope to meet sometime and thank Him for His gift to me."

"What's that?" Brian asked excitedly.

"The gift of life, Brian. The same one you want to give to Louie but you can't. Louie can only be a mirror of you just like we are all mirrors of God. I don't know God very well at all. I'm afraid to say your dad and I haven't given much thought to God in our own lives. We don't read the Bible and the last time we went in a church was for your grandfather's funeral, but still I know how I was raised and I've never heard an explanation since that made more sense to me. We were created in God's image and likeness. It doesn't mean God has a head and hands and walks around on two feet. What it does mean is that our souls are mirrors of God. We communicate, we love, we feel, it's what's inside us that makes us like God. Brian, everyday you come home you go up to your room to work on Louie. It's time you get out, meet some kids, make friends, because when the right person for you comes along, you're not going to be able to take advantage of meeting her. You're not going to know how to communicate. Brian, Louie will probably never be finished. Just like none of us are ever really finished, we all have our shortcomings that we are always trying to work on. Why don't you join a sports team, the debating club, student council, anything. Get to know some of your peers. Believe me, in the long run, it'll do you a lot more good."

CHAPTER THREE

THE GROWING YEARS

Puberty has a magnetic effect on both sexes. Boys notice girls, girls notice boys, children who couldn't be dragged by military police to the showers and tubs discover perfumes, make-up, deodorants, and colognes. Brian Phillips was hit full force with puberty.

The summer before his thirteenth birthday, he packed up Louie and some of his test equipment and piled into his parents' four-by-four for the yearly pilgrimage to Martha's Vineyard. Their house, though not directly on the cliff, overlooked the cape and was only a few blocks from the East Chop Beach Club. Brian had several acquaintances in school that were girls, but none he had given any thought to. He loved his mom, but that was alright. She wasn't really a girl, she was his mom—vastly different.

That morning he left Louie in his bedroom looking over the cape and headed out to the beach club to sail his little sunfish. He was a good enough swimmer that his parents didn't mind him going out alone as long as he didn't go too far from the shore. He skidded to a stop on the sand-covered path that led to the shed where the sails were kept. Then he saw her, Alice Newman, a petite blond with big blue eyes. He felt his heart racing and his palms begin to sweat.

"Hi," she said, extending her hand, "I'm just here visiting my aunt and uncle. You really know how to ride that bike, don't you?"

"Yeah," Brian responded, nearly choking on his tongue, "I guess I do."

"You going out sailing?" she asked.

"Yeah, but there's room if you'd like to come along," Brian responded, wondering what she'd say.

"I don't know if I should, I'm not that good of a swimmer. I heard those little boats can capsize real easily."

"We've got some extra vests," he said, extending his hand. "I'm Brian. My folks let me go out by myself. I'm a pretty good swimmer. Here, see if this vest fits you."

The nervousness was gone and Brian set out to teach Alice all about sailing, tacking, getting the most out of the wind, and how to correctly read the waves. They were out for almost three hours when Brian saw his mother waving to him from shore.

"Looks like my mom must want me to come back in," he smiled. "What do you think, do you like it?"

"It's heavenly," Alice said. "I can't believe how quiet it is out here. Don't you hate going back into all the noise and people shouting?"

"No, my parents don't shout and Louie doesn't either."

"Louie?" she asked curiously. "Who's Louie?"

"I'm a computer designer—robots. Louie's a robot I made from a lobster I caught. He's the greatest. He can speak a bunch of different languages and answer almost any question you could throw at him."

"Oh, kind of like a talking Chatty. You ask Louie a question and he says yes or no?"

"No, much more than that. Why don't you come over after dinner and I'll let you meet him. Who's that there?" Brian asked, pointing to the beach.

"Oh that's my Uncle Bob. He's such a worrier. My cousin Emily died last year in a freak car wreck up in New Hampshire. Now he worries about everybody. He's the one who probably told your mom to wave us in."

As they pulled the sunfish onto the beach, Uncle Bob walked over. "Alice, don't you think that's a little dangerous out there? You hardly know how to swim. What if you capsized?"

"Hi, Uncle Bob. This is Brian. You know his mom and dad, don't you?"

"Yes, hi Brian. Did you know she can hardly swim?"

Brian looked at him like he was stupid. "Yeah, that's why we're wearing life jackets. I really can sail and we didn't tip over."

"Uncle Bob, he showed me how to come about, read the wind. Brian's a great sailor. Please don't say I can't go out again. I'm sorry I didn't ask you first, but it's so beautiful out there." Alice kissed him on the cheek.

"Well, you can go out again. I guess it's all right but don't put such a scare into me. I didn't have the faintest idea where you were. Why don't you two come up to the snack bar? I'll buy you some hamburgers. You've got to be hungry. It's almost one o'clock. How about it, Brian? Do you want to join us?"

"Sure, I'm just going to put the sails away and say hello to my folks. I'll be right up."

Brian rolled the sails up and put them back in their nylon sack. He marvelled how easy it had been getting to know Alice. He wondered if God had ever made a prettier girl. He searched his memory but couldn't recall having ever seen one he thought was better looking than Alice. He smiled at his good fortune and decided he had really worked up an appetite.

The summer went by the speed of a hurricane wind. It was over before Brian had even know it had begun. Louie went from being his best friend to being something he was proud to show off, and Alice couldn't have been more fascinated. Several times they had taken Louie into Oak Bluffs and had him talking to people on their way in to Mad Martha's Ice Cream parlor. People would look around puzzled and Alice and Brian would laugh their heads off when people realized that they had been talking to a robotic lobster.

Finally the day came when Alice had to say goodbye. She was going back to Shipley, New Hampshire where her dad ran a successful tavern. She hadn't told Brian much else about her family. Brian went to the airport to see her off, and before she got on the plane, he snuck his first kiss. They exchanged addresses and promised to write. That night Brian had no appetite and picked over the roast chicken that his mom made him, normally his favorite. The food seemed to have taken on a leathery taste.

"Come on, Brian," his mom said, "at least try and eat your food."

"Brenda," his father said, "I think he misses his friend, Alice." Then addressing his attention to his son, "Look, Brian, that's the way life is. You enjoy people while they are in your life. Nobody knows how long someone is going to be with you. She was a real nice girl but you're young and there'll be other girls."

"Dad," Brian interjected, "she's really the only friend I've ever had, I mean, besides you, mom and Louie. It feels like something inside of me like died. Do you know what I mean? She's only been gone a few hours and already I really, really miss her. What am I supposed to do? I hurt inside."

"Brenda, Brian and I are going to go for a walk on the beach. I don't think we'll be doing much more eating. Why don't you put everything away? We'll have cold chicken tomorrow."

Brian and his dad hopped into the Jeep and went to the lighthouse park at the end of the street. They parked, got out, and walked through the tall grass.

"You know, son," his dad said, "nothing at all can stop you from hurting. It's a sign from God that you're really alive. When you have to worry is when you don't hurt anymore. Old King Solomon said, 'There's a time for laughter and a time for sorrow.' You're young and your heart is strong, but sorrow is just as much a part of life as is joy. That's why as much as you love your experiments with robots, they'll never ever be alive. I mean, they can talk to you in every language known to man, answer every question, even joke around with you, help you with your work, but they can never love you, Brian, and that's what makes us different from them. We feel, we love."

"Dad, I don't understand. It's not like I ever decided to love her. Where does it come from?"

"It comes from God. It's how we know that we were made in His image and likeness. God is love. All love comes from him. Alice left and you miss her. You miss having someone to share your thoughts with, your dreams of who and what you are. She understood and you loved her for it. Treasure the memories and stay in touch with her. Love can survive over great distances. Remember that you don't have to be with someone to love them. The feelings of love permeate this very universe we live in—not mathematics, quantum physics, astronomy, but love. You see those stars up there? They serve no other purpose for us except to show us God's love. Mankind will never travel to one of them. We know that the light from them left for our planet eons ago. But God put them there to remind us of how much He loves us. That pain you feel in your heart for Alice, well, that's a fire, a light of how much you care for her. Whenever you get a chance, you let her see it and it'll make her feel better too."

That night was to change Brian's life forever. No longer would he be a recluse hiding from his fellow students, afraid to love, afraid of rejection. He knew that whatever life had to offer he was going to square his shoulders and look each day straight in the eye and accept all of the challenges. The years passed and Brian grew closer to Alice as they spent more summers together. He returned to school a healthy sixteen-year-old to finish his senior year.

Brian was unanimously voted the president of the debating club. He had met a few of the kids in the club studying in the library and had been ever reluctant to join, but his relationship with Alice had bridged the span between him and the rest of his peers. It gave him a new boost of confidence that he was quick to take advantage of.

He was a natural at debating, storing information, and it was a breeze to repeat it in context. He tirelessly poured through the research material before each debate and practiced his performance in front of his closet mirror. He versed himself with both sides of the issues and found the holes in his opponent's arguments.

"Well," his dad said, "when you finally graduate, what do you want to do?"

"I want to keep working with artificial intelligence. I think I can make a real impact."

"Do you want to live here and go to MIT?" his mom asked.

"Yeah, I'd like to but with Dad and everything being around, it might be better to get out on my own. Well, I'd really like to go to Stanford. I know it's a long way off, but I can come back for the summers."

"What does Alice think?" his mom asked.

"She wants to go to Stanford too, but it's going to be a while until she gets out of high school. She's got another year to go," Brian said.

"Well, your mom and I are very proud of you, and wherever you want to go is fine with us. I'd like you to come to MIT but you've got to make your own way. We're behind you 100%. We'll be here for you," his father said, shaking his hand.

It was decided, because of his excellent performance in the national debating finals, Stanford had already offered Brian a full ride scholarship to begin after the summer. That spring before he graduated, he determined to forget about debating and computers. He would just appreciate Alice and his last truly free time.

It had been three months since they had visited together, and Brian couldn't believe his eyes when he saw her. She had begun to fill out and grew more and more beautiful. When he saw her running up the beach towards him, he thought his chest was going to explode.

"Alice!" He gave her an awkward hug. Then he leaned back to kiss her. "I missed . . ."

She kissed him back before he could even finish his sentence.

"I know," she stated matter-of-factly, "I've missed you too. So sailor, you going to take me sailing?"

They pulled the boat out and headed toward Vineyard Haven around the lighthouse, enjoying every minute of each other's company—talking about college, debating the latest advancements in medicine and computers. There was never a dull moment between them. They passed a sleek black yacht with a helicopter on board and some beautiful people on the deck.

"That's what I'm going to have when I'm rich and famous," Brian stated.

"Any room for me in your dreams?" Alice asked.

"Yeah, you can captain my yacht," Brian laughed, getting himself doused with a handful of saltwater.

They finished out the day at the tennis club where Alice had taught Brian some of the fundamentals beating him soundly every game. She was amazed that he allowed himself to get beat so completely without even a protest.

The next day when he got up, he felt so fully alive, it was as if every feeling hidden within him came to full blossom. They sailed the whole week up and down the coast and one day they barely missed being sucked in by the undertow from the huge passenger ferries transporting the tourists from Vineyard Haven to Wood's Hole.

As their friendship grew, the intimacy grew between them. Alice had strong religious and moral views on premarital sex. Although they exchanged long, passion-filled embraces and deep kisses, everything else was off limits. It didn't matter to either of them; they were inseparable. Little by little Alice began to explain to Brian why she believed in a God and what her relationship to Jesus Christ meant to her. Brian had hundreds of questions about the suffering of the world, men's free will, predestination, good and evil, and why man was created. Alice, although she was not as skilled in debating as Brian, answered his questions honestly and let her true self shine through.

"Brian, it's not enough just to acknowledge that there is a God. In the Bible it says even the devil believes in a God. You have to dedicate your life to Him, make Him your Lord."

"Alice, that sounds sort of medieval—God as a Lord? What are we? His serfs to roam through His earth rescuing damsels in distress?" He looked at her and knew he had hurt her feelings. "I'm sorry."

"It's not my feelings that are hurt, Brian," she stated matter-of-factly. "It's God's. He wants to be your friend. He wants you to enjoy this beautiful creation, but He also wants you to give credit where credit is due."

"Like pay the piper."

"No, more than that. You give Him your life, He gives you His," she looked at him imploringly. "Brian, I know I don't talk that much about it. I've never been that good at sharing my faith, but I've really thought about it and I know I owe it to you. When you were born, you were born into sin. No one taught you how to steal or lie and be selfish. These are all things that come to us by nature, but they separate us from God."

"How? God knows we're like that. I mean, He created us. Why does it matter to Him?" Brian asked.

"Because God is perfect and someone that is imperfect and full of sin can't be associated with Him. It's simple. He wants us to live forever with Him in Heaven and to do that, we have to be cleansed of those things that are different from His nature of love. Anything that is not love for Him—yourself or your fellow man—is sin."

"How do I get rid of my sin?" Brian questioned. "It's not like I consciously chose to be like this. You just said it was how I've been born. What can I do to shake it off?" Brian, for the first time, was perplexed.

Alice explained to him about the payment for mankind's sins by Jesus Christ, his resurrection from the dead on the third day, and the Bible. She explained how different she was after she accepted Christ. She asked him if he wanted what she had. He did.

That afternoon they sat up by the lighthouse overlooking the Cape and Brian asked Jesus Christ to be the Lord of his life. Inside he felt a current of energy surging through his veins. He couldn't wait to get home and tell his mom and dad what had happened.

The reaction that he got was totally opposite from what he expected. Instead of his parents being glad that he found God, they reacted quite coldly.

"That's great," his mom said. "I'm glad you and Alice have forged a common bond. But really, I think you should just keep it to yourself. When I grew up there were three things you never discussed: your religion, how much money you make, and politics."

"Sounds pretty boring when you grew up, Mom," Brian added. "But heck, if you don't want me talking about it, okay, no problem. It was a total rush, like when I asked God to forgive me. It was like this fountain went off inside of me. You can't imagine how it made me feel. It's really hard to explain. How come you and Dad really never have that much to do with God?"

"It's not that we don't have anything to do with God, we just didn't want to push anything on you."

"Why not?" Brian asked. "What if I would have died before I got forgiven by Him? I never would have gotten to spend eternity with Him."

"Who told you that, Alice?" his mom asked. "That's not necessarily so."

"Sure it is, Mom. It makes perfect sense. It's like God lives in this perfectly clean environment, like those clean rooms they make computer chips in. Anything that is dirty that comes in and pollutes it really can't exist with God. He needs the perfection around Him to keep Creation working in perfect harmony. I never really saw it before. Alice pointed it out. There's always been something about myself that I didn't like. No matter what good grades I get or how hard I try, I just can't be perfect. I mean there is no way. There was something wrong with me, Mom. At my very core something really, really wrong. Do you understand at all what I'm saying?"

Brian's dad entered the kitchen carrying a box with three lobsters. "Hi, Brenda. Hi, Brian. You like my friends?" his dad joked. "They're not quite as clever as Louie. Obviously if they were, they wouldn't be in this predicament. What's wrong with you two?"

"John, Brian and I were discussing God," Brenda said. "It seems that Brian has discovered that he needs salvation and he prayed with Alice to accept Jesus Christ."

A crease passed on John's forehead as he set the lobsters down.

"Is that true, Brian? You prayed to Jesus. Something missing in your life?" his father jested. "I mean, you're practically 16."

"Dad, I know you don't talk much about Jesus Christ, but don't you ever wonder? Suppose you're wrong and He really is God. Don't you want to get to know Him even a little bit?"

"No," his father stated. "There is a God, but I don't suppose He's much concerned about what's happening down here. I mean, it seems like maybe he's on a permanent vacation and has just left us to make the best out of a bad situation. He's not someone I'd go putting a lot of confidence in. To love is to know God, son. And there are a lot of other people who claimed to know God besides Jesus Christ."

"John, there's no reason to be so harsh with him. Believing in Jesus Christ is certainly not going to do him any harm." Brenda reached over and took the lobsters and began boiling the water. "Why don't we just leave him alone? Maybe some day he'll forget all about it."

"I think there is. Brian's got to learn someday to stand on his own two feet. He's going into the real world. In case you've forgotten, Brenda, in a short time he'll be living in Palo Alto, California. Our little boy is leaving home and it seems like he's exchanging his real parents for a Heavenly Father. Isn't that how it goes? Our Father who art in Heaven. Haven't I been a good enough father to you, Brian? You really need some mythical Heavenly One to fill some void in your life?"

"No, Dad, it's not like that at all," Brian was on the verge of tears. "I am not too good at explaining it—not like Alice anyway. But when I made Louie, I made him like I wanted him to be. I programmed him, Dad. I made him responsive to my voice and for a while I really believed that he was talking back to me. If someone found Louie and saw what he could do, they would have known almost immediately that someone had a hand in inventing him. What about me, Dad? I mean you're my biological father but do you really think you created me? I was programmed too out of your's and Mom's gene pool—chromosomes—so many for a male, so many for a female, X and Y. Who was the programmer? You expect me not to believe in a God, a Higher Power who actively cares about us when I see how complex we are. Dad, in case you forget, I've been trying to create life myself, things that are real that can move, talk and live. I haven't been able to. No one has. Artificial intelligence is just that: it's artificial, not the real thing. You and I and Mom are the real thing." Brian reached over and picked up the lobster. It tried to snap at him. "This is the real thing, Dad. Louie isn't. I'm the real thing, Dad. I needed to know who made me, why I was created. From you, Dad, I got my love for inventing things for computers. I've got the greatest parents any kid in the world could want, but I know you didn't design me. God picked who I would be. You couldn't have even chosen if I'd be male or female. You didn't know how tall I'd be or what color of eyes or hair. Those were all things that God decided when I came to life. If I really want to find out what I'm supposed to do with my life, I want to find out before I spin my wheels and go out half cocked as some kind of mad scientist. Look what happened to Albert Einstein. Do you think he was happy inventing the atom bomb? I don't think so. Try and be a little bit fair. I won't push my new beliefs on you, but please don't push your lack of beliefs on me either. You're the only dad I'll have. Sure, I have a Heavenly Father, but it was He that chose you as my earthly father. Don't push me away just because you don't want anything to do with God."

* * * * *

In the Circle of Light the guardians were still rejoicing that Brian had accepted the rule of the Mighty One in his heart. An unending stream of pure light flowed from the outstretched hands and wings of the Gods of War as they sang and worshipped their Creator. The streets in the Circle of Light were thicker than a larger glacier, yet translucently gold. Gold refined beyond all metallic properties so all that was visible were the very purest of atoms in a total liquid state. The huge pearls that framed the outer gate of the New Jerusalem were carved into Corinthian columns larger than even the largest redwood tree. Raphael had just returned from planet earth where he had been monitoring the conversion of Brian.

"Oh lofty Mighty One," Raphael thundered, "what is your wish? Just tell me and I will do your bidding. What are your plans on behalf of this one you love?"

"Raphael, your very presence brings me unspeakable joy. There are many who wish to use Brian's talents for evil. Even now they plot to destroy the good he can do for his fellow men. You must be his guardian. You must keep his feet able to walk my path and to bind off those who would hamper the purposes that I have for him. Even now the evil ones work within him to discourage. The very humans who brought him into the world now seek to discourage him and keep him from fulfilling my purposes. Go my faithful messenger and make a way for him in Palo Alto. Arrange so other of my followers may be around him and guide him in the right direction."

"Mighty One, your wisdom is the wisdom of all ages, the light that forever guides us through the darkness, the voice of peace in a tumult of cacophony. May I make a request, Oh Mighty One?" Raphael bowed before The Presence.

"Yes, you may state your request, for I know your request," the Mighty One replied.

"Uzziah has served before your throne tending the eternal flame with the oil of your people's sacrifices. Perhaps, Mighty One, you would allow him to accompany me. It is lonely out of Your presence. How I miss your circle when I am wandering to and fro on the earth. I carry within my being Your Eternal Light, yet the darkness on the earth from the fallen ones is so great sometimes . . ."

"Raphael, Uzziah shall accompany you that you may not feel the separation, for this journey is to be a long one and it will be a while till you are again in my presence. Take heart, I will be looking forward to the time when you bring your charge into my presence. Remember, Raphael, Santero wishes again to bring the humans into a bondage that they might be subject to him and him alone. I see all that he plans, yet I know mine and I shall not allow anything to take them out of my hands. You are mine, Raphael, and I shall not suffer anyone to defeat you. Come closer," the Mighty One beckoned.

Raphael drew close, accompanied by Uzziah, much smaller in stature. Uzziah's wings were short, his hair a fiery red down to his waist. His eyes were the most peaceful of blues with a complexion bronzed by the burning of the oil day and night for endless time. As they drew close, they linked together and knelt before the Mighty One. The Son rose from His spot next to the Mighty One and spoke.

As He reached out, the power flowed from Him through two holes in His hands. His voice was calming and brought silence to all. "My faithful messengers, how I felt your presence when I walked among men. I felt your sorrow as you watched me crucified. I know, Raphael, that you would have taken me off the cross and carried me back here to be healed, but that is in times past. I am the Lamb slain from the foundation of the world, the Lamb slain so the children of Adam may come before this throne like you do in purity of heart and soul. The pain of those we created is never out of my heart. I bear the memories and the scars forever and ever. It is not my wish that the children of men should perish but they might taste my goodness, a goodness so encompassing that when they taste of it, they shall never be satisfied with the fruits of the world." Jesus reached out with his hands and touched Raphael and Uzziah. "I have given you power to aid my witnesses that my message may go forth on every country on the earth. Go now, guide this young man that he may stop those who seek to bring my brothers and sisters into eternal bondage and torment."

Uzziah and Raphael were unable to kneel; they found themselves floating away. It was as if a river had caught them up. They soared together through the blackness of space and came to rest outside of the Phillips house where they encountered the first of the evil ones.

Sawtooth was blacker than pitch-black darkness. His mouth opened in a jagged array of glistening daggers. The only thing not black was his eyes, a deep crimson, that seemed to flow forth with sulphur. He carried on his person the smell of pungent sulphur, and at first breath, Uzziah found himself gasping, having been used to the sweet oil that burned before the throne.

"Raphael," Sawtooth mocked, "what brings you here—or do I have to guess? I suggest whatever it is, you leave. We control this family, and have for the last three generations."

"That's too bad," Raphael retorted. "Uzziah and I have been assigned to their son Brian, or maybe you haven't heard. He's joined us. We're his guardians. Maybe it's time to return to your fire, or don't you have fond memories of it? The minions screaming and begging you for water."

The pores on the back of Sawtooth's hands oozed with a black liquid and his mouth dripped with froth. He drew out his dagger and flipped it from palm to palm. He drew himself up to full height, towering over Uzziah. Faster than the eye could see, he slashed out at Uzziah. Raphael drew his wings over Uzziah and thwarted off the blow, and with a gust of wind from his mouth, blew Sawtooth head over heels into the air.

"Be gone," Raphael bellowed, "into the tormenting fire . . ."

"Noooooooo," Sawtooth screamed in terror as the earth opened below him and he plunged into the pungent darkness.

Raphael and Uzziah checked out the Phillips residence to see if any other of the fallen were lingering around. The entire mood of the house changed with their presence. A few moments later they were checking the residence for any hidden presence, they sensed Ballelulia coming up the walk with Alice.

Uzziah, having been nearly cut to shreds, was happy to see his former commander.

"Greeting in the name of the Most High Ballelulia," Uzziah beamed, grasping Ballelulia around the shoulders.

"Praise be to His wonderful name, Uzziah, and you also, commander Raphael. So the Lord of Hosts sent both of you?" Ballelulia inquired.

"Yes, we're to be the guardians for Brian Phillips. Apparently the Lord Most High has some wonderful plans for him as He does for all of His children," Raphael responded. "It has been a while since I have walked among men. It pleases me to see you and your charge, Alice. I believe she was the one that showed our charge Brian the way."

"Yes, Coontobo tried to thwart her but her prayers persisted and I was able to bind him," Ballelulia beamed. "I'm sure he is stoking the brimstone or has met the wrath of his lord Santero. He was most reluctant to depart. He kept encouraging her to hide her testimony for fear of rejection."

"I'm sure it must have been a challenge for you, Ballelulia," Uzziah interjected. "From what I've been taught of mankind, the battles of the mind are the most difficult of all."

"Indeed, guardian Uzziah, they are indeed. Are you here as an apprentice to commander Raphael? Do you not miss being a keeper of the eternal flame?" Ballelulia asked with concern.

"Yes, I do miss being an attendant to the Mighty One," Uzziah responded sadly.

"In all fairness, Ballelulia, it was I who asked the Mighty One for his company," Raphael pointed to Alice. "We have been sent to prepare the way for Brian Phillips in Stanford. Do you know whether she's joining him?"

"Yes, she plans to, but she must finish her high school first. I know why the Mighty One died for these poor humans. Some of them are so precious. You should hear the prayer of this one. All day long she prays and shares love with everyone. It's all I can do to keep my feet on the ground. The many attacks that she comes under from her uncle and aunt are most easily thwarted." Ballelulia pulled his sword and did a dazzling twirling and shadow parry. "The fallen ones stay away from my charge. That is, unless they enjoy being maimed."

"Commander Ballelulia, I pray to the Mighty One that I should be able to handle my sword as well as you handle yours. I stand humbly in your presence," Uzziah bowed.

"Thank you for the compliment, host Uzziah, but power and glory to the Lord of Lords. It is the prayers of my charge to whom I owe my expertise and skill. You will learn, Uzziah, that your strength comes alone from those to whom you are entrusted and your strength will rise and ebb even as their spiritual health rises and ebbs. I have learned to speak to Alice and encourage her to pray for herself and for others. She has responded and now my power in this realm has grown. May my success be an example to you," Ballelulia bowed.

"Mom, Dad!" Brian shouted as he grabbed his windbreaker. "Alice is here. We're going to ride our bikes down to Mad Martha's for some ice cream and maybe go to the video arcade, okay?"

"Sure," his dad responded. "Don't be back too late."

The path down to town was strewn with rocks and Ballelulia and Uzziah were busy removing the rocks out the way so their humans didn't tumble and break their necks. Brian threw caution away and bolted down the small, winding hill, almost running head on into an oncoming motorist. Ballelulia grabbed his handlebars and pulled him off to the side while Uzziah watched in amazement.

"Uzziah," Ballelulia said, "you've got to stay ahead of him, behind him, and try to anticipate his every move. Otherwise, he's dead."

"I don't know," Uzziah said. "I sure wish Raphael hadn't just left for Palo Alto."

"No," Ballelulia reassured, "don't sweat it. It gets to be second nature after a while. Don't let one incident bother you. This happens almost five to ten times a day. You have car accidents, poisoned food, falling meteors, lightning, earthquakes, suicidal tendencies, drug overdoses, murders, airplane engine malfunctions, train derailments. Guardians can anticipate all of them. It's important to keep your eyes and ears open. That way none of these things will catch you unaware."

"Will you show me, please, Ballelulia?" Uzziah implored. "I'm new at this. It's nothing like tending the eternal flame. Who would have ever thought it could be so challenging."

"Yes, certainly I'll show you," Ballelulia said. "In a few days you'll have it down pat."

CHAPTER FOUR

THE FIRE BELOW

As Sawtooth descended into the vast whirlpool of darkness, the billows of sulfuric smoke permeated his nostrils, causing him to gasp for breath. He struggled with the cord that Raphael had entangled him in and found that the more he tried to remove it, the tighter it got.

His eyes quickly adjusted to the darkness and he could make out the shadows of those who were imbedded in the molten lava and his ears tuned into their woeful cries for help. "Fools," he thought. "All of them had exchanged the wisdom and love for their Father Creator and swallowed the pack of lies taught to them by Santero and the fallen."

As he landed on the shore of the Lake of Fire, he laughed scornfully and approached Delmondo, who was throwing another pleading soul into the lake.

"No, please," the young girl screamed, "this can't be happening to me. I don't believe in Hell. This can't possibly be real. It's not fair. Wait! Send me back. I'll repent, I'll go to church. I'll help the poor. I promise I'll do anything. Just let me go back."

"It's too late," Delmondo replied. "Your fate is in our hands. Scream all you will. You can't undo what's been done. You spurned the love and forgiveness of the Mighty One and now your body and soul belongs only to us. No one else shall have you. You think he can hear your cries? The Mighty One has turned His face from you. You will see Him just once when you stand before Him in judgment." His talons ripped into her and she found herself launched over the lake. She came down in hot, molten lava and was buried up to her neck.

"Noooooooooo, I'm burning . . ." she cried. "Please God Ooooooooooooh someone help me, pleeeeeeeeeeeeease."

The sound provoked laughter from Delmondo and he turned to look at Sawtooth.

"Back for your old job, Sawtooth? Oh, I see you met one of the Gods of War. Looks like you were no match," Delmondo ridiculed.

"Save your comments and untie me from these cursed light bands. They strangle the very life force within me. The pain is immense." Sawtooth turned and Delmondo sliced through the light band which turned into nothingness. "Maybe you should take your turn on the surface. This constant wailing grows very tiresome for me. It must grow heavy to you as well."

"No, not at all, really," Delmondo snarled. "I've grown quite used to their pleadings. I've met very few that embraced this Eternal Fire. Most have been quite unbelieving up until the very moment they arrive. There are many more of us down here now. We've expanded the famine areas and increased the drug overdoses. It's as busy now as it was during the heyday of World War II. Everyday with each unwitting soul, the lake grows larger and larger. It doesn't make any sense. I would have thought by now the souls would be stacked on top of one another, but instead, they seem to grow more and more distant."

"Well," Sawtooth replied. "I'm sure Lord Master Prince of Darkness, the Eternal Wrath, will require my presence to explain my failure. He cannot bear the thought that we are not all-powerful as the Mighty One and the Warriors. I guess it's appropriate that the Father of Lies lives a lie as well."

The passageway down to the Royal Chamber wound round and round as if it were a never-ending corkscrew. The wall grew closer and closer together. As Sawtooth neared the abode of Santero, Lord of the Underworld, the ringing of chains grew louder and louder. It was to be one of the few times Sawtooth would speak directly to Santero. He knew the summons would not be pleasant and he feared for his blackened hide. Before he got into the chamber, he stopped and watched the line of captive souls marching before Santero and his laughing cohorts. Periodically they would pick groups destined for the Lake of Fire and allow them to grovel at their feet, making a mockery of them.

* * * * *

It was a day that never seemed to end for her. Connie had been raised in the finest home in Grosse Point, Michigan. They had a large English tudor style house with plenty of old money to send her and her sisters to the finest private schools. They had all attended Sunday School until their mom had decided to dump their father and live the wild life. She never recovered from the bitterness she felt toward her dad for abandoning her, even though she later found out her mom had made it impossible for him to see her or her sisters. Her mom had used the family money to effectively lock her father out of guiding the family. It was shortly after that time that Connie lost her virginity on the family room pool table and started drinking and smoking pot.

It was never enough for Connie. There was always an emptiness. She tried to fill the void with shopping sprees, buying new outfits of the finest silks and linens from the most expensive designers: handmade Joan and David shoes, DKNY silk pants, expensive soft leather garments. She justified her drinking by comparing herself to real alcoholics who were living on skid row, and even though she had watched her wealthy grandmother die in an alcoholic stupor, she vowed that it would never get her.

One drink was never enough for good-time Connie. Seven and sevens, imported beer. Her milk-white skin began to lose its elasticity and her nose, petite at first, began to enlarge and grow bulbous as the circulation in her extremities began to suffer the punishments of continual alcoholic abuse.

Friend after friend came to her begging her to quit drinking. She seemed to bounce back time after time. Only 95 pounds, she

Friend after friend came to her begging her to quit drinking. She seemed to bounce back time after time. Only 95 pounds, she could hold more alcohol than most fully grown men. Many times she'd wake up the next day having blacked out, not even knowing how she managed to get home. Her sisters were the same way, so she never thought that what she was doing was even a little out of the ordinary. One day while driving home from her community service job, she stopped at the fanciest place in town and allowed some of the regulars to buy her a few for the road. Being a woman in control, she liked to spend her money on others as well. She had to buy them a few too. By the time nine o'clock rolled around, she was well past inebriation. Nobody said anything to her when she got up, put on her coat, and headed out the parking lot where she had parked her new Jaguar. She figured she wasn't that drunk. After all, she was able to negotiate the key into door and get her car started. She pulled out on Camelback Road, one of the busiest streets in her hometown, Phoenix. She didn't even see the Yellow Freight truck heading the opposite way. He couldn't stop and all ten tons of his vehicle and trailer demolished her. She was killed on impact, never even realizing who had hit her.

The fallen were in the shadows waiting for her. Demoncolies and Rubio deliberately distracted her so she'd be hit. Before her spirit could even leave her body, they had chained her. She struggled and protested, but it was to no avail.

"What?" Connie said as she rose above the wreck of the car and viewed her human host body lying mangled. "That can't be me. I'm too young. Wait!" she yelled as Rubio bound her wrists. "Get that chain off of me."

"You're coming with us, Connie," Demoncolies said. "It looks like you had one drink too many. Bottoms up," he taunted as he lifted her feet first, bound like a calf in a rodeo, and proceeded to drag her screaming through the asphalt into the hollow earth.

She was puzzled, but the Mighty One had given her many, many chances. She had seen the best evangelists the world had ever produced speak to her. She dated a man who prayed and fasted for her soul ever day for over a year. Instead of letting her heart get soft toward God, she continued to harden it. She claimed God wasn't interested in her, had nothing to do with her life, and she didn't want to hear anything about Him. Like a fool, she figured she had plenty of time. After all, she was only 25. Time to party, make love, get high, see the world, get drunk, live it up. There'd be plenty of time later to make things right.

As they dragged her through the sediment into the molten center of the earth of the Lake of Fire, she wished she had listened to those who tried to warn her. She was beyond fear. Her white Jaguar, plush townhouse, imported shoes, handbags, linen outfits, and million dollar trust fund lost all importance. She wished she had taken the time to really listen to the warnings of those she labeled as fanatics and weirdos. Religion was great for them, but not for her. It was for old people—people who lacked self-confidence. She realized how wrong she was. She struggled with the chains hoping to somehow escape, go back to earth, and live her life over again doing what was right. She realized that it was hopeless, that she had forever chosen her destiny.

She began to smell the smoke from the fire below. It reminded her of the volcano she had visited with her sister when they vacationed in Hawaii, where she had gotten so high on the local marijuana that she forgot even where she was. She was broken hearted. She thought about her sisters, her mother, her father, her stepbrothers, and friends, and wished she could somehow get a message to them so they wouldn't have to suffer the same fate she was suffering. She thought about all the time she had spent reading *Cosmopolitan* articles on sex with boyfriends and the latest fashions, the times she had wasted watching *Cheers* and wished she had taken time to get to know the Creator who had gone to the cross to save her and everyone else from the Devil's torment. It was too late, she knew, but she wished she could do it all over again.

There were several others with her chained together as they marched her before Santero.

"Well, Connie," Santero queried, running his fingernails down her stomach, wounding her, "do you like your new home?"

"Look," Connie pleaded, "I really never bargained for this. I spent a lot of my time helping people. I visited rape victims, gave money, and things to poor people. I was usually a pretty good person. Look, there's a hell of a lot of people who did many worse things than me. How about letting me go back?"

"Yes," Santero chuckled, "I figured you'd have something interesting to say. What's the matter? Don't our accommodations seem to agree with you?"

"I didn't figure there was really anything after death," Connie said hopefully. "I figured when you were dead, you were dead. End of the story. Look, what do you need me for anyway? I'm sure you've got plenty of people down here. Give me a break. Let me go back, just to tell my sisters and mom."

"No," Santero said, "I don't think that's possible. You had a certain appointed time to live your life and now it's up. Your going back isn't going to change anything for your sisters either. They have to live with their decisions as well."

Connie became desperate. She threw herself at Santero's scaly, oversized feet and wrapped her arms around them. "I'll do anything you want me to. Anything—just let me go back and warn my sisters, please!"

"Sorry," Santero smiled smugly, "you've already done exactly what I wanted you to do. You're here, aren't you? I'm sure we'll get to know each other very well." Santero reached in her mouth and pulled out her tongue. "As for now I'm tired of hearing you speak."

Cadaver chuckled, grabbed Connie by the ankles, and pitched her into the Lake of Fire where she landed head first. It didn't matter, either way the torment was more than she could bear. There was no choice. She had to bear the torture. Worst of all was the mental anguish, the knowing that what she was going through was senseless.

Carl Maduri watched in horror as they tormented Connie. He was hoping to talk his way out of Hell altogether. At age 15 he started buying wrecked cars from insurance companies. He did the body work and paint himself and took the chassis to have them straightened. Of course, no one that he ever sold them to suspected that they were totaled-out vehicles. They just thought they were getting a great buy from a stupid kid. He never let on any differently.

He parlayed the money he made selling cars into a first-class education at the University of Iowa. While not attending class, he opened his own used car lot and began selling barely operable cars to other students. He put them on contracts that were interest heavy, and when anyone was over 30 days late with a payment, had the car repossessed in the middle of the night. The beautiful thing to him was, he could sell the same car over and over and over again. One 1978 Camero he was able to sell 12 times. With the money he made, he speculated in the commodities market, getting tips from local farmers and ranchers on corn and pork bellies. By the time he graduated, he was worth several million. It wasn't quite enough. He moved to Des Moines when he bought into a Toyota dealership and then eventually five other different dealerships as well as rental agencies. He married the model who did the television commercials for him and then he started to raise his own family. Church and God were at the bottom of his list. He worked six days a week and Sunday mornings found him at the golf course or in the winter at the rifle range. Julie belonged to the First Church of the Nazarene and would complain about the example he set for the children.

"You've got to set the example, Carl," she exclaimed while holding Timothy, their youngest. "Our kids aren't going to want to be going to church if they don't see you going as well."

"I'll go next week," he'd lie. Anything to get her to leave him alone. "We've got some of the people in from Tokyo. I'm up for the new Isuzu dealership. I told them I'd take them to the club."

The time never came. He'd hear his conscience telling him to slow down. There were other things in life besides the next deal, but he was hooked. At first he wanted to retire at 40 with 10 million in the bank, live off the investment interest, but then it became a matter of pride to be able to leave his sons with the businesses. Mike, Steve, and Tim were the pride of his life. He didn't care whether or not they went to church. He only wanted them to follow in his footsteps.

Being always in a rush, he didn't eat very well. Coffee and a sweet roll for breakfast, chips and some barbecue for lunch, and then he'd head home for a big steak dinner. He grew fat and his heart grew weaker and weaker as it struggled to keep pumping blood to his ever-increasing physique. It was on the fifteenth hole at Garner Country Club that it gave out. He remembered it so well. He laid the first shot on the par four in the middle of the fairway about 270 yards up. He loved his new Ping driver. It was a dog leg left with another 35 to the green. His partner, Doug Honiker, sliced it so Carl grabbed his five and six irons.

"You take the cart," he told Doug. "I'll walk up. God knows I need the exercise," he joked. Fat jokes no longer bothered him. He was fat and he was rich. What the hell did he care what people thought about him. Seven car dealerships, net worth of over 20 million, and a wife that would put Vanna White from "Wheel of Fortune" to shame. He never got to hit the green and go for a birdie put. About a hundred yards from his ball, he clutched his chest and fell forward from a massive coronary. He never recovered. They worked on him for over 90 minutes. Thirty-one years old.

At first he sort of floated around his body, watching all the commotion, until he figured out it was him lying on the fairway. Through the trees he could see two wraith-like black beings. Their eyes were red and he could hear chains rattling. He looked around to see who they were after, and it dawned on him that they were after him. He tried to enter back into his body but couldn't.

"You're ours," Detenmento sneered at him through a mouthful of blackened, decaying teeth. "These are for you," he held up the chains, laughing.

"You've got to be making a mistake. I'm married, I've got businesses to run, a wife, three kids, over 800 people working for me. I'm a multi-millionaire. This is some kind of joke? Right," Carl reasoned.

"It's no joke, dude," Incendiary said as smoke poured out of his mouth. "We're the real thing. These chains are for you, Carl."

He tried to struggle, but obviously they were masters of the their unseen domain. As he felt himself being pulled through the earth into the molten center, he reasoned that he'd be able to talk their boss into letting him go back. Now he found himself face to face with Santero and didn't have the faintest idea what to say to him.

"Well, well," Cadaver grimaced, "who have we here? Carl Maduri. Well, Carl, you did quite a good job for us making money, good employees, Christmas parties, plenty of free booze, nice women you hired for the visiting Japanese, even yourself a time or two. And yes, you made quite a mark with the substandard brake and repair jobs your companies did. I understand you don't think it's quite your time. Am I right?"

"Well," Carl stuttered. For the first time he was really, really worried. No one to bail him out. "It's just that I have a lot going for me back there. Why's it gotta end now? I just turned 31. I was thinking maybe you grabbed the wrong person."

"Ha ha ha," Santero sauntered over, playing with Carl's large, extended stomach. "Quite a healthy appetite you had? Huge little fat boy." A large stone was rammed into his stomach. "Here, this will give you a little more weight as you enjoy your swim in our beautiful lake." His stomach was weighted down and he struggled away from Santero right into the waiting hands of Cadaver. He found himself being grasped painfully and Cadaver's hands burned through him causing him to shriek with pain. He was hurled a seemingly endless distance and watched the people below him stuck in molten lava up to their necks seeming to go mad in the tormenting fire. Before he landed, he realized he had made a serious judgment error by putting his accumulation of wealth ahead of the pursuit of salvation. It was hopeless. He knew he was doomed forever. He just hoped his wife and children wouldn't suffer the same fate. Not just one deal but an eternity lost.

Amanda Singer cowered in the background hoping to escape the notice of Santero. Her chains didn't seem that annoying. She had put chains on plenty of men while on earth. Born in Cincinnati, Ohio, she had discovered just how beautiful she was at age 14 when her stepdad had run away with her, divorcing her 35-year-old mom and marrying her before a Justice of the Peace across the river in Kentucky. Until then, she had always felt inferior to her mother. Life had been a constant battle out of her mom's shadow. Growing into puberty had made her feel quite like an ugly duckling, but by age 16, she had all the attention she could want. Lance Wolford, her stepdad/husband, had more money than he knew what to do with. He insisted that Amanda get silicone implants to increase the size of her breasts. She was reluctant at first, but bathed in the attention she got from men and women alike, especially waterskiing in the summer. By 18, she found herself quite bored with Lance and the rest of her life. Without saying a word, while Lance was in Chicago tending to his family's large publishing business, she packed up and moved to Orlando where she got a job at the Pink Pussycat, one of a chain of topless bars run by the Lebanese Kaseem brothers. She was in much demand as a dancer and moonlighted out of the club pulling in an easy thousand for private performances. They began to feature her in their advertising, and she decided to have additional implants done that increased her breast size to over 48". It was a lot of extra weight to carry around and made it difficult for her to sleep at night except on her back, but she was glad to be rid of Lance, her stepmom, and making her own money. After buying the condo with a lake-side view, a leather interior Lexus, and making a couple of trips to the Bahamas, she began to plan her future. Through her dancing she met George Underwood, an investment broker who helped her parlay her 10 grand a week into a varied portfolio that earned her anywhere from 11 to 15 percent, mostly tax free. After a year in business, she had socked away about $300,000.

Every week on her way to work, she passed a huge church, the Orlando Christian Center. She wondered to herself what would be so interesting about church that they would have to build such a large structure to hold so many people. She had met her share of religious people. Many had kinky habits or were plain voyeurs, giggling over her body and lusting after her. One Sunday morning, out of curiosity, she went to the church. She wore dark sunglasses and dressed down in a fairly baggy overcoat to hide her massive implants. She was touched by the sincerity of the message and the testimonies of healing and salvation. She woke up from what seemed to her to be a dream, only to find herself standing in front of the platform. A young lady wearing an altar worker name tag came over to her and put her hands on her shoulders. Amanda was sobbing uncontrollably.

"You don't have to carry your own burdens," the altar worker said to her. "It says in the Bible that He Himself bore our sins. Cast them at the feet of Jesus. You can leave here today a new person, all the old things passed away."

Inside she heard for the first time a really clear, small, mesmerizing voice that bore testimony to the truths the altar worker was speaking. "Do it. Do it," the voice kept saying.

She turned to look at the altar worker and noticed the name tag, Sarah Kennedy. "How can I turned from my sins? I make my living as a stripper. Everything I have is because of that. Look at me," she sobbed. "I've made myself into a freak of nature so that men could ogle me and pay me. What am I supposed to do for a living?"

The girl at the altar was taken aback. She searched for words to respond with, but none were forthcoming. Amanda got up without saying another word. She knew there was no place in God's Kingdom for her. Four weeks later she was dead from a freak boating accident, and now she realized for the first time how crazy she was not to have walked away from her dancing job to follow Christ. She saw the other side and it was grotesque. Cadaver wandered over to her.

"Amanda Singer, my, you were a hit for us," Santero snarled, wrapping his hands around her neck, squeezing it. She found the squeeze pass right through her.

"Look," Amanda tried to explain, "I was stupid. I had my chance. Send me back. Give me one more shot. I'll make up for what I did."

"It's not what you did, Amanda," Santero addressed her, "it's what you didn't do. You had your chance to bail out of the life of sin permanently with no record, and still you chose your own way. I'm curious, why? We made but one mistake, and yet we were banished for eternity, but you could have accepted forgiveness for all of them. Yet, you held onto them like they were your long lost friends. Was your life as a dancer that rewarding? Did your luxuries mean so much to you down there that you bartered a few years of pleasure for an eternity of grief?"

She knew the answer. She had been foolish beyond measure, deceived by riches. Now her eyes were open, but it was too late. She had drawn her last straw. She remembered sinking to the bottom of the lake, slowly drowning and thinking how peaceful it was going to be until the Fallen Ones had drugged her out of her slumber and brought her to this living Hell. There was no sense in answering Santero, she thought. She knew she'd be cast into the Lake of Fire for an eternity. She began to sob uncontrollably and that sobbing was never to stop.

CHAPTER FIVE

DECISIONS, DECISIONS, DECISIONS

His sixteenth birthday came and went so fast, Brian thought he'd never recover from the events. When he woke up that morning, September 1, he was handed a set of car keys and his bathrobe by his excited father. He knew that they were planning on getting him a car to drive to Stanford in Palo Alto, but he didn't have the faintest idea what kind. He had visualized himself driving a vintage Toyota with a busted radio or maybe a used Volkswagen van. He wasn't prepared for what he saw in the driveway. There, under the rusted basketball hoop, was the most amazing car he had ever seen. The Dodge Stealth aerodynamically perfect in fire engine red.

"Well, what do you think?" his dad asked.

"Dad, I'm sorry, but that's got to be the dumbest question that anyone has ever asked me. This is amazing. Can you really afford to be this extravagant?" Brian asked.

"Well, we saved your whole life for your college education and you're going on a full-ride scholarship. What else could we have done with your college earnings? It's yours," his dad beamed. "It will even talk to you if you don't fasten your seat belt or forget to close the door. Your mom and I thought it would be perfect. What do you think? Shall we take it for a spin?"

"Yeah," Brian responded. He hopped in and pushed the automatic lock button, letting his dad in. The engine jumped to life and Brian could feel the power pulsating under him. One hundred sixty horsepower, rack and pinion steering, Brian felt like he was driving in the Daytona 500. It was six o'clock on a Sunday morning and the streets were nearly empty. He shifted gears twice and was doing 55 in seconds. When he shifted to third, the rpms were still running low at 70, in fourth to 95, and he watched his dad turn a little white as he hit a hundred. "This is unbelievable, Dad," he said, checking his rear view mirror for any highway patrolmen looking to fill their ticket quotas.

"Don't worry about police, son," his dad said. "We took the liberty of installing a radar detector. Just don't get any tickets. Insurance on this is going to be running us over $2,400 per year. The agent thought we were crazy buying it, but you know how it is."

They spun around in the car for about 30 minutes and pulled into Dunkin Donuts where Brian ordered a coconut cream and his dad had a bran muffin and coffee. They went back home where they pulled in and went in the house. His mom was still sleeping and Brian immediately picked up the phone to call Alice. She was sleeping, so he told her stepmom to wake her up. It was important.

"Hi, Brian," Alice said, trying to shake the sleepiness from between her ears. "You didn't have to call me. I know it's your birthday. I really was going to call you. Happy birthday. What's up?"

"You won't believe what my folks bought for me for college. It's amazing. I've never seen anything like it in my whole life," Brian was gushing with excitement. "I just wish you could be here right now. I'd love for you to see it."

"What is it? Will you slow down and just tell me?" Alice never could stand surprises.

"A car, a red car. It's the most amazing thing I've ever seen." Brian was beside himself.

"Brian, that's great. I'm glad your parents bought you a red car. But there are hundreds of different types of cars. What year? Who made it? Do you think since you've called me at seven o'clock on a Sunday morning and I don't have to be up for at least another hour and a half you could at least tell me what kind of car?" Alice was puzzled. She knew Brian was a bit of a space cadet, but had never known him to just space out details. Whatever it was, she was sure that he must have found it to be pretty astounding.

"Wait, I'm sorry. I don't remember the name. Just hold it right there. I'm going to go and check." Brian set down the phone. Still in his slippers, he ran outside and looked on the side of the car where it said Dodge Stealth. He ran back into the house and picked up the phone.

"Alice, you still there?" he said, a little short on breath.

"Yes, I didn't hang up on you," she half joked. "Have you figured out any more details? I mean, Brian, a red car. That's pretty sketchy, especially for a stickler like you."

"It's a Dodge Stealth. It looks like a rocket ship. Like one of those vehicles Luke Skywalker fought the empire with—a starfighter. It's amazing, it's so fast. I could get in it and probably be there to visit you in an hour. It goes up to 180—probably faster." He was out of breath.

"Wow." Alice was speechless. "That's incredible." She felt a tinge of jealousy as she reflected on her '81 Chevy Nova in rust brown with its AM only radio sitting outside her window. "That sounds like it must have cost a fortune. Will you drive it up to see me? You know my stepmonster won't let me go down again till school's out. She doesn't think it's right, me running off to visit a boy."

"Yeah," Brian gulped, "I mean I'll ask my mom and dad. After all, I'm going to have to drive it across the country at the end of the summer. They're not going to mind me driving it to New Hampshire, surely. How about if I come up next month on a Friday after school? Can I stay with your neighbor, Bart Thomas? Do you think you could ask him?"

Alice knew Bart had a big crush on her and would do anything for her. She also knew her stepmother would never go for Brian staying in the same house with her. They were religious to a tee without any flexibility that makes religion more enjoyable and life better. They had the crust without the bread.

"Bart won't care," Alice stated. "You know he asked me to his senior prom." She paused, letting it sink in. "I told him no—not even as friends," Alice lowered her voice. "I told him I was in love with a mad scientist and that if I ever so much as thought of cheating on you, you'd fix it so my life was a walking nightmare."

"Not quite, Alice. Really, you could have gone. I don't want you missing all the fun parts of school because I live so far away, but if you kissed him I'd sedate you when you were sleeping, open up your cerebral cortex, and fix it so the rest of your life you'd have an uncontrollable drool. Your friends would call you Alice the drooler. We'd have to get you a bib to wear. Anyway, I really should get off the phone. After all, it's long distance, and with that car, I'm sure my parents got set back a little financially. No point in adding any additional economic burdens," Brian stated matter-of-factly.

"So, you're really going to come up," Alice choked. "I miss you so much, I don't know if I can really wait. It's going to be the longest month of my life. I love you."

"I love you too," Brian repeated.

* * * * *

Ballelulia, the warrior assigned to Alice by celestial standards, had a pretty easy time. Alice had let her imagination wander and desperately wanted to leave her stepmother and father and start her own family. At 17 she felt she was pretty much ready. She had full confidence in the power of her love for Brian. It was magical ointment that would somehow smooth away every problem.

As Alice's mind wandered, she allowed her spiritual strength to ebb. No longer would she spend hours talking to the Mighty One or reading from the Holy Scripture. Instead, her time was spent daydreaming of the home she'd share one day with Brian when he made his millions from the computer business. She thought of how she'd show everybody, including her dad and her stepmom, that she could do quite well, thank you, without them.

Her daily communications to the Mighty One became quick moments before meals, thoughts while in the shower, and momentary prayers said while gazing into the stars. There was no longer any deep sense of communication, where she would spend hours just enjoying the lingering presence of the Mighty One which had overshadowed her life for so long. It wasn't that the Mighty One withdrew His presence from her. It was that she had ceased to go around it. At 17, she was the most beautiful girl that had ever walked the hallways of Franklin Roosevelt High in Shipley, New Hampshire. All the kids had grown up with her, so only the newcomers were awed by her beauty. Everybody else just accepted her as Alice in Wonderland. Most of them thought she probably did drugs, the way she walked through the hallways, oblivious to everything around her. They didn't know that it was love of another kind that had captivated her so.

She hardly noticed herself ebbing; it was so gradual. Her stepmom left one week with no explanation, and that same Friday her friend, Jeannie, from the homecoming committee, asked her over for a party. With Brian so far away, she decided to go. Jeannie's mom and dad were divorced, and her dad made his living as a rep for a large shoe company from Dexter, Maine, so he was barely home. But when he did come home it was usually to a pretty well-stocked liquor cabinet. He drank so much, he didn't even notice how weak the liquor was.

"Hi, Alice," Jeannie giggled as she let Alice in.

"Dad gone again?" Alice asked.

"Yeah," Jeannie laughed. "You thirsty?" she said, holding up a mug of frothy pink. "Strawberry daiquiris. They're great."

"What's in it?" Alice asked.

"Here," Jeannie stretched out the glass to her, "have a sip."

Alice tasted and licked the forth from her upper lip. "Is there alcohol in here?"

"Yeah, not much, though. Isn't it sweet?" Jeannie walked into the kitchen and picked up the pitcher she had just made. "There's plenty."

She didn't even try to go home. Two glasses and she was pretty much history. She called her dad and said he would be up late and would he mind if she stayed over at Jeannie's. He didn't. The next morning she woke up, her mouth was dry and her temple was throbbing like she needed a root canal.

"Hi, Alice," Jeannie said cheerfully. "What's wrong, you have a headache?"

"I don't remember much from last night. Where did I get this groaty sweatshirt? My head, it's still throbbing."

"Don't sweat it," Jeannie counseled. "Everybody feels that way the first time they get drunk."

"Great," Alice said, "I was drunk. On your strawberry drinks?"

"Yeah," Jeannie replied, "I didn't realize you had never drank before. Like you have no tolerance. You looked really funny sort of stumbling around."

That was the first time that Alice imbibed on the vine. She kept telling herself that it was all right, that she wasn't an alcoholic. She started carrying a small flask of vodka to school and emptied it into her Coke can at lunch time. Hardly anyone noticed, and she grew more and more forward with people. Several times, when on the phone to Brian, she slurred her words and explained it away by saying she was tired. Brian was beginning to catch on.

* * * * *

Bibliontec was ugly by anyone's standards. Invisible to the human eye, his presence still sent chills down spines throughout the universe. His skin was a greenish tint covered with boils, and his nose was elongated and hooked at the end. His ears were overgrown, elephant shaped, and his hands resembled cloven goats' hooves. His feet were also cloven. His hair was a fiery orange and his size was impressive. He carried chains with him that he used to bind his human victims. He had bound Alice to her addiction to alcohol and enjoyed being able to plant thoughts in her head anytime he wanted. He was making preparation for the visit by Raphael. He had already subdued Alice's guardian Ballelulia.

"You won't be able to deal with Raphael and Uzziah as you've dealt with me, Bibliontec. His human still knows the power of prayer," Ballelulia spoke with authority.

"Save your speeches for someone you can torment, Ballelulia. You weren't guardian enough to keep your charge from falling into my hands. I'll increase her appetite until her kidneys are irreparably harmed and her liver is gone as well. Another yellow-skinned creature living the last years of her life tied to a machine and hating the Mighty One for what He has done to her," he laughed uproariously.

"You think taking advantage of a child's ignorance makes you powerful. You're worse than your master Santero. You look only to corrupt," Ballelulia pleaded. "Why don't you just depart, leave her alone? She is not causing your kingdom any harm. She is of no value to you whatsoever."

"Maybe now she isn't," Bibliontec retorted. "But there will be a time when she will be. Besides, we like to get them started young when they are ignorant and know no better. Stop your pleading, Mighty One of Valor. Where is the Ballelulia that helped topple the walls of Jericho? You surely don't look the warrior of old. Your present situation is indeed pitiful. What is the matter? Couldn't the Mighty One give you an assignment worthy of you? Are you reduced as well to guarding little girls? Even in this you have failed."

"Maybe I have failed, or maybe not. It is not my actions that are judged but hers, and that by One who is all-merciful and all-powerful and alone knows the end of every situation. Don't be so smug in thinking that you have reached a victory when in fact you may have reached none at all. Only one knows her outcome. Yes, I have had more grand assignments than the one I am on presently, but perhaps this shall turn out to be a grand experience as well. I know that I have come to love my charge and will do all within the power and place allowed to me. Don't think I won't receive help. And as far as past assignments, if you consider the destruction of Marilyn Monroe and Jim Morrison crowning achievements, then indeed your thinking is as corrupt as your own vile presence. Yes, Bibliontec, I remember you in your former glory when you sat near Octonoo basking in the glory of the Mighty One. You were not a misshapen creature that couldn't decide whether to be man or animal, as you have become now. I may be saddened by Alice's use of alcohol and her lying, but not nearly as saddened as reflecting on your past glorious carriage and seeing what you have become. Don't you ever long for the courts of the Mighty One, the crystal sea, the healing leaves? Don't you miss the light? Do you wish forever to dwell in outer darkness in the tormenting flames?"

"It is you and your Mighty One that shall be cast out of the Circle of Light. Santero has promised us complete and total victory, and these chains that we use for our human victims shall be used for you and the Mighty One. Though He may have made the world and the universe we live in, the Mighty One has failed miserably in giving us free will. We have used our free will against him and shall triumph. Think of how many more are cast into Hell than enter the Circle of Light. Do you not think that we have the victory already? How many worship at Mecca and call Mohammed their prophet and Allah their only God? Does it not make the followers of the Mighty One look like a tiny minority?

Before you boast, Ballelulia, know what you boast about. Your Mighty One may still enjoy his glorious throne, but it will not be forever. The outer darkness that He has chosen to cast us into will surely be His eternal abode. So it is that I should caution you about remaining on the side that will indeed be vanquished. We are many, we are powerful. We are legion."

* * * * *

Right after calculus, Brian hit the road for Shipley. It was the longest month he could remember. He was already light years ahead of his teacher in the realm of comprehension and Mr. Murdock was more than happy to let him leave after he finished the test, which was exactly three minutes after he got it.

He pulled out of the parking lot and onto State Route 57, which took him to the outskirts of Boston, where he caught 222, which Brian had calculated to be the quickest way to Shipley. Brian didn't have the faintest idea that Alice had developed a drinking habit and that, in fact, just one month she had become an alcoholic. His intelligence was great for theorizing, but not well experienced to deal with real life problems. He loved the feel of the road and pushed the gas pedal down until he was doing over 130.

Raphael and Uzziah were not affected in the least by speed. They were used to traveling beyond even the speed of light, in a dimension unknown to most humans as superconductivity, the dimension of love. They served Brian as the result of a directly command of the Mighty One, but they loved the Mighty One so much that they also served Brian out of love. It made it easy for him to respond to almost every situation. They never questioned why he had been given what appeared to such a lowly assignment instead of guarding a president or well-known evangelist. He accepted his appointment with joy. They could see into another dimension, the dimension of life and earth. Like all the Gods of War, he was instinctively alerted whenever a human was close to death or on the verge of ascending or descending to eternity. Santero was not inclined to play by any rules, and if he could snatch even those saved in the blood of Jesus Christ and drag them to torment, he would have. Fortunately, it never happened. Guardians were always present to guide the followers to the Circle of Light where all would rejoice.

"Warrior Raphael," Rufel sang, "I bring you greetings from the Lord of Hosts. They are planning an ambush for you when you arrive in Shipley. The enemy has set a foothold through your charge's girlfriend. Beware Raphael, keep him with all diligence."

"Are there any to assist us?" Raphael questioned, "or are we to go alone?"

"Unfortunately," Rufel sadly responded, "none have prayed for the area and the darkness is great. We have not been able to penetrate the area. Even the radio waves are forbidden to us. Your friend Ballelulia has been rendered nearly powerless. We wish you the best. Many of the young ones are being recruited for a cult of devil worshippers. There have even been sacrifices of newborn babies and animals. You cannot go through the town without seeing signs for fortune tellers and liquor stores. It truly is a dark town."

"Is there not even one church that has given itself to pray for our help and deliverance?" Raphael pleaded. "Surely this is not India. This is the United States. IN GOD WE TRUST."

"Would there be that there was one, we could go and deliver these foolhardy souls from their impending destruction and damnation," Rufel responded. "The only church there was splintered several months back and the minister is an alcoholic. It is worse than in the times of Noah."

"Thank you for the warning. All praise and honor be to the Mighty One," Raphael sang.

The law of love ruled the Circle of Light. An unseen dimension fueled the guardians' concern for those they were assigned to protect, that they would have given their own lives to save their assignments. Ballelulia felt nothing but love for Alice. As he saw her getting hooked on alcohol, starting to lie, and beginning to curse, his heart was panged with sadness.

He was used to the dimension of love where the Mighty One caused all to dwell completely in His love. As Ballelulia watched Alice have a drink in preparation for her visit from Brian, he reflected on what the Mighty One had told all of them about the flow of the universe.

"What you feel around you, the substance that flows through your very being, is the essence of the Universe. It is what all matter is made of and what all seen and unseen consists of. It is my general great love and desire for all beings that I have created to enjoy my presence. In your assignments on the Earth you will surely grow saddened while you are away, but I instruct you now to know that I am with you always. Everywhere you go and everything you do, indeed, I am with you. Nothing can remove you from my hand. Though the Evil One and his minions should wrap their chains around you and hinder you from aiding those to whom you have been assigned, I am with you. My gift of love is the very source of life. Should you need to touch someone who is sick or of broken spirit, remember it is my gift of love that will transform them. Should you need to find some way to comfort someone who is hurting, remember that it is my gift of love that will comfort them. I am sending you out as my guardians, but I am equipping you for your assignment. Love is all you'll need. It will suffice for each and every situation."

Alice walked to her dad's fully stocked bar and poured another Seven and Seven, telling herself that she didn't really need one but that she was nervous about Brian coming up for the weekend. Alice had no idea why so many in her town drank and were alcoholics. She figured it was like that everywhere and didn't know its true origin. Only a small portion of New Hampshire runs near the Atlantic Ocean. After the purge of witches in Salem in the 1600s, Sarah Brougham had come up to Shipley with her three sons, Terence, Maynard, and Thomas. To make ends meet, they built their own small distillery and had sold liquor to the sailors who would come to Shipley for a time of R & R. Unknown to them, other spirits came as well. Ballelulia set up residency as well as a host of the fallen. With the liquor plenteous and cheap, they made sure everyone imbibed. Many of the descendants of the liquor magnates could trace their origin to Shipley, New Hampshire. In many places, their old houses stood like huge mausoleums on top of beautiful verdant pastures, deserted as the descendants had moved to warmer climates like West Palm Beach and the Carolinas.

Shipley was one town where you didn't have to worry about getting a ticket for drunk driving. The police barely patrolled the streets. They were too busy playing pool and drinking nearly every night themselves. Even the mayor was known to have been carried to his house many nights, too drunk to even remember where he lived. Alice's father operated the most successful bar, The Wise Owl Tavern, known for its unusual atmosphere. Tourists stopped to see the famous moving shot glasses which occasionally fell off the bar under their own volition. Peter Townsend had made profits beyond measure selling low-quality booze, which he poured after hours into expensive bottles, making a cool 1000% profit. It was of no concern to him whether or not Alice drank or what she drank. In fact, he would have preferred she drink rather than follow some crazy religion.

"Alice," Peter cried out. "Oh, there you are," he said as he wandered into the den and saw her putting away one of his liquor bottles. "Don't worry, a little whiskey never hurt anybody. Pour me one, will you."

"What'll it be?" Alice asked coolly.

"What are you drinking?" Peter responded.

"Seven and Sevens," Alice said proudly.

"Just the Seagrams for me. Say, isn't this the weekend your friend is coming from Boston—that computer whiz of yours?" Peter asked.

"Yeah, he's on his way right now. Don't worry, he's not staying here. He'll be staying next door."

"Why, isn't our home good enough for him?" Peter asked, pounding his shot down.

"Dad, don't you remember, mom didn't want him staying here."

"Nonsense," Peter said. "Of course he'll stay here. We don't want your friend imposing on a neighbor. We have more than enough room here. I've got to be getting back to the bar. We've got a great crowd. Why don't you bring what's his name again?"

"Brian, Dad," Alice said in a hurt manner. "His name is Brian. I've been dating him for almost two years."

"Well, whatever," Peter slobbered, "bring him down too. We'd love to have him."

"Dad, I don't think he's ever had a drink," Alice persisted. "I probably shouldn't either."

"Nonsense, don't believe everything you read. Ever since the beginning of time people have been drinking spirits. You wouldn't be living in this nice house if people didn't drink. It's not all bad."

"Dad, I'm going up to get ready. If Brian comes, please be nice to him, will you? Don't show him your whole Jim Beam bottle collection. He probably won't care."

CHAPTER SIX

SHIPLEY

As Brian pulled off Route 22, he wound the Stealth up the road past ancient seaside Victorian houses. Most were in pretty rundown condition. The place resembled an old, abandoned Welsh coal town. The trees looked skeletal with the full moon blooming through them. It only accented just how bare it looked. The street lamps were the old-fashioned kind from the '20s that had been converted to electricity, although several were out. He bounced into a few pot holes that sent him up into the roof of his car and caused his compact disk player to skip a few songs on his Magic Man CD. He couldn't explain the coldness that seemed to permeate his bones, leaving him with an empty, hollow feeling.

He pulled out the directions to Alice's house and pulled over to the side of the road to read them. A pickup truck, full of middle-aged men wearing Pendleton shirts that barely covered their beer guts, pulled alongside him.

"You lost, son?" the passenger asked, sporting one missing tooth, with the others decayed entirely beyond recognition.

"No," Brian said, "just checking directions. You know if this road intersects with Whitehaven?"

The man laughed. His stomach shook under his red plaid shirt. "You're on Whitehaven. What are you looking for? It's a small town where everybody knows everybody."

"I'm looking for Alice Townsend's place. You know it?" Brian inquired.

"Peter Townsend's daughter—she's a mighty fine one. That's probably why you drove all the way up here in that fancy car. Looks like a rocket ship. Sure, I know it—fifth house on the left. You can't miss it. There's a great big iron fence around it. They say years ago someone died on that fence and old man Seagram just left him hanging there. Nobody on the fence now. I s'pect you can drive right on up to the house. Come by the tavern later. We'd like to get more acquainted with you, maybe even buy you a beer."

The pickup truck sped off and Brian just shook his head in wonderment, puzzled at what kind of town Alice lived in. He looked over to his right and noticed the Apostolic Tempe. He recognized it as the church Alice talked about all the time. He pulled up and looked at the marquis out front. It read:

EASTER MORNING SERVICE 9:30

He thought it was odd that it was the end of September and they hadn't changed the marquis. He made a mental note to check with Alice. The outside of the Townsend estate was indeed impressive. Brian couldn't recall ever having seen a house so massive. The driveway was at least a hundred yards long, made of cobblestone with towering bushes on each side. As he pulled to the front, he noticed the large, Grecian marble fountain and the massive columns blending Corinthian and old Colonial architecture. The gate creaked as he let himself in. Peter, dressed in corduroy and a red wool vest, opened the door.

"Welcome, you must be Brian. I'm Alice's dad, Peter."

Brian extended his hand and walked in. "Nice to meet you. Alice has told me a lot about you and her stepmom."

"Well, I'm afraid Harriet isn't here right now."

"Is she away on business?" Brian asked cordially.

"Not exactly. The circumstances of her leaving are rather unpleasant and I'd rather not go into them. Perhaps Alice will feel free to disclose them to you later on. Can I get you something to drink? A martini, perhaps?"

"A Coke would be great. It's a long drive up here," Brian commented. "This is the most beautiful house I've ever been in. Some people in town told me it was the old Seagram estate."

"Yes," Peter answered and pointed to an old oil painting hanging over the fireplace. "That's Cyrus Seagram there. He's my great great great great grandfather. The only thing we share in common is the cleft on our chins. I don't have the fortune he had. The trust money skipped my generation. I'm in the same business, but I just operate a tavern restaurant—The Wise Owl."

"That's certainly a catchy name," Brian added. "Neither of my folks are much for drinking. I guess I'm not much either."

"Excuse me for a second. Here's your Coke. I'm going upstairs to get Alice."

As Peter ascended the great circular staircase, Brian looked around. He felt as if he was in a museum. Everything was so old. The lighting was dim with stained-glass sconces, the carpet was beautiful, but very threadworn. The smell was musky.

"What brings you to our fine city, Raphael?" Bibliontec taunted. "You and your kind have not been welcome here for years. These people belong to us—always have and always will. We are their spirits."

"Where is Ballelulia?" Raphael directed, touching the hilt of his weapon. "Perhaps you should look for another to taunt. I have little patience with the fallen. And as far as this town belonging to you, the earth is the Lord's and everything therein. Perhaps you should start packing."

Raphael looked up and saw Ballelulia descending the steps after Alice. "Ballelulia, what is wrong?" Raphael queried.

"Alice has quit praying altogether and barely acknowledges the existence of the Mighty One any longer. Her stepmother ran off with Reverend Jacobs from the Apostolic Church. She has turned her back in bitterness. This entire town is vile. You will hardly find one sober soul.

It is true. I am the only guardian here. I have grown very weak, Lord Raphael."

"Be of good cheer, Ballelulia. The Mighty One will not forsake us, though there be a thousand against us. We are to look up, for our redemption will draw night. My charge has memorized the entire New Testament and knows how to use the Word of God like a sword. Look at how sharp mine is."

The light from his weapon was blinding. It lit up the room like a train headlight would shine in a dark tunnel.

"Put that blasted thing away. Even you, glorious Raphael, can't defeat our power here. We have been entrenched here far too long," Bibliontec scoffed.

"We'll see," Uzziah spoke. "The Lord reigns here too."

"Alice, you look great," Brian cried.

Alice ran down and nearly jumped into his arms. "Oh, Brian, you're here. The most awful thing happened this week. I couldn't call you and tell you or I know you wouldn't have driven up."

"What? I mean you're still alive. Nothing that bad could have happened. Let's sit down and talk. Is your friend Bart still expecting me to stay at his house?" Brian asked.

"No, my stepmother's left for good—moved out," Alice began sobbing.

"I heard. Your dad told me," Brian said, putting his hand on her shoulder and drawing her closer to him.

"She ran off with Reverend Jacobs." Alice looked at him mournfully. "Brian, I've been drinking everyday since she's been gone. It feels so bad, I just want to numb the pain."

"It's not the way to do it, Alice. The scriptures say we are to 'cast our cares upon Him, for He careth for us.' Not to be drunk with wine. Alice, Jesus knows the pain you are in. He'll deliver you and he can bring your mom to her senses as well. All we need to do is really pray for her and the Reverend Jacobs. Just because somebody goes off the deep end doesn't mean they have to drown, if two or more people agree. Just you and I, Alice, we can pray and watch the Mighty One change the world."

Ballelulia began to recover his strength as Alice repented of her drunkenness and sought forgiveness and restoration for her stepmother and pastor. The golden color returned to his face and he began to dance about with joy and expectation.

"Shall we bring them back, Lord Raphael? I have heard they were staying just up the road near the tavern," Ballelulia said.

"Yes, indeed, we shall."

The Shipley Inn was a seedy place. Many shingles were missing from the roof, and only the EN was working on the OPEN sign. Harriet Townsend was in room 6 with Reverend Jacobs. They were on a binge and were both miserable.

The affair had started with Harriet going to Jacobs for counseling, and had progressed to them drinking together. They eventually fell into immorality. The congregation at the Apostolic Temple dwindled to nothing until neither of them cared anymore who knew about the affair. Jacobs felt his career was over and had drifted into an alcoholic stupor, only briefly interrupting it to engage in adultery with Harriet and to shove down a hamburger or two.

Across town, Brian had an idea. "Alice I can't explain it. Is there a motel here called the Shipley Inn?"

"Yeah, why would you know about that?" Alice queried.

"I've got sort of a sixth sense that maybe we should go there. That's where we'll find your stepmom." Brian looked at her seriously, "We should definitely pray before we go over there. I sense a real evil about the place."

Uzziah had whispered to Brian the name of the motel. "You don't mind that I told him, do you Commander Raphael?" Uzziah asked.

"No, not at all, Ballelulia. There's just the three of us. Have you any idea how many of the fallen are residing around the motel?"

"I think there are legions. That motel has been used for immorality and drunkenness since it has been constructed. It's a permanent residence for coke addicts as well," Ballelulia added. "I hope these two can really pray. We are going to need the power to march in and set these captives free."

Brian grasped Alice's hand and they dropped down to their knees next to an old Victorian fainting couch. The room was lit by an old Gone With the Wind lamp which cast faint shadows. In earnestness they began to touch the Mighty One with pleas of mercy for the minister and Alice's stepmom.

"Oh Mighty One," Alice implored, "forgive me for not being a better example to my stepmom for always rebelling and not respecting and loving her as I did my own mother, for making her feel like an outsider in our own home and looking down on her, telling her I didn't belong to her, and she had no right to tell me anything. I'm sorry. Set her free, Oh Lord, from this alcoholic spirit and spirit of adultery that has her bound. Set her free, Oh Lord, bring wisdom into her life that she may do what is good and acceptable in your sight." Alice began to sob and Brian put his arms around her shoulders.

"Dearest, Lord Jesus, Maker of Heaven and Earth, Creator of all, Lord of the Universe, all knowing, all loving Holy One, we are not worthy of Your great blessing, yet You call us Your friends. You have said to agree to ask together and Your will would be done on earth even as it is done in heaven. We agree together here and now that this minister and Alice's stepmom should have their eyes open to their sins and should forsake their sins and turn to You. Oh God, don't hold this ignorance against them, but deal with them from Your bountiful mercy, not according to their sins. Give us the power to speak Your word to them and see them set free. We ask humbly in the name of all names—Jesus Christ."

The burden passed out of the hands of Brian and Alice and they nearly floated outside to the car. Their guardians stood taller and glowed with a presence that could nearly be felt, "the touch of angel's wings," as songwriters had written. They were going to the Shipley Motel full of compassion and mercy to deliver a warning to those who were in danger of perishing—a warning that they believed would be heeded and would turn the minister and stepmother from the path of damnation to salvation.

"Turn left here," Alice pointed. "If you take this side street, it's not very far, maybe two minutes."

Ahead of them, unseen Ballelulia, Uzziah, and Raphael flew towards their showdown. In the realm of the unseen, the bondage of the motel was clearly visible. The motel was draped with chains of darkness linked over as if it were mosquito netting. The fallen were lounging indolently, not expecting company. Ballelulia struck the first chain, sending it falling and bringing out a snarling being.

"Who dares sever my chain?" Ichobod cackled. "I'll have you roasting."

Ichobod, as black as the night with green, glowing eyes and a hairdo that resembled the Cat in the Hat, checked himself when he saw the guardians.

"What have we here?" he gloated. "The white knights to the rescue. Aren't we brave? The three musketeers coming to save some damsel in distress. Well you all must have taken the wrong turn somewhere in the solar system. There is absolutely no one here worthy of being saved. So why don't you save us a lot of effort and go back to your cursed Mighty One?"

"Ichobod," Raphael changed, "you know we can't do that. Summon your legion if you must, or if you'd rather, just go away cowering. That option is open as well. As you see, we are not on a social call. We come in the name of the Lord of Lords, the Mighty One. We mean to bring an end to the captivity of two that you have entrapped in alcoholism and adultery."

Raphael drew his sword; it was blinding. Just as Ichobod tried to call out for help, he found himself beheaded, unable to make a sound.

"You should have turned aside." He stared down pitifully and remembered Ichobod from the Circle of Light where he tended the Mighty One, bringing fresh coals of worship before Him. It gladdened Raphael to dispose of the fallen. He knew that although he stripped them of their power, they always returned at another time, still serving the Lord of Darkness.

"Before the others awake from their lechery, we should free Harriet and Reverend Jacobs," Uzziah exclaimed.

"Let's be off!" Raphael responded.

The door to the motel room was guarded by a huge, slothlike being. Gordiuoso was over 15 feet high and as round as a redwood tree. His skin was a pickled green with red welts and nostrils that were as wide as a man's fist. He was sleeping and barely woke as he felt the chains being cut.

"What?" Gordiuoso stammered.

"Step aside," Uzziah exclaimed. "We are claiming these two back."

Uzziah twirled his sword with lightning speed and cut Gordiuoso's arms off at the socket before he could draw his huge mace and pummel them all.

"You filthy warriors," Gordiuoso cried. "That's not fair."

"Those who sleep must return to the deep," Ballelulia cried. "Return, oh giant one to the Lake of Eternal Darkness."

Ballelulia took a light rope and threw it over Gordiuoso's throat, choking off any sound, and spun him into the air, hurling him eons away.

Alice knocked lightly at the door. "Mom, is that you in there? It's me. Open up, will you?" She tried the door and found it open.

Harriet was fast asleep, an empty glass with a cigarette floating, next to her. Reverend Jacobs was wearing a tank top t-shirt and baggy boxer shorts. The Gideon Bible was next to him as well as a nearly empty Jose Cuervo tequila bottle.

"I'll get the Reverend dressed,' Brian said. "You wake up your mom."

It took Alice a while to get her stepmom up. When she finally came to, she looked surprised to see her stepdaughter.

"Alice," Harriet mumbled, "who let you in? You're not supposed to see this. Who put you up to this, your father? No, couldn't be him. He could care less."

"Mom, I love you. I know this is a weird time to say it, but I don't think I ever gave you a chance to really be my mother. You always tried so hard and I was so, so cruel to you. I came here to tell you I'm sorry. I want you to come back home. I know what you've been doing, but I really believe we can work everything out," Alice said imploringly. "I really need you, Mom. I'm only 17. I don't want to live the rest of my life without you. Please!"

Harriet began to weep. At first, only out of the corner of her eye a little dribble fell, then there was a torrent. As Alice held her, she could feel the convulsions, the wracking pain of someone who has gone to the very bottom of emotion only to find the emptiness, and yet the promise of love and forgiveness.

"How could you love me, Alice?" Harriet asked. I'm such a bad role model here in this room with our minister. How can I ever even look myself in the mirror again?"

"Mom, even King David sinned with Bathsheba. God forgave him, and He'll forgive you too," Alice explained. "I really need you, Mom. This is no kind of life for you."

"You're right," Harried said. "Let me get my things. Who is in the bathroom with the Reverend?"

"Brian. He really is a great guy, Mom," Alice beamed. "You're going to love him."

When Alice, Harriet, and Brian returned home, they found her father passed out on the couch. Alice pushed him on the shoulders.

"Dad, wake up." She leaned closer. "Dad, Mom's back." She instinctively took his pulse. His arm was stiff, unlike anything she had ever felt. "Brian," she asked, "come here, my dad's . . . something's wrong."

"Better call an ambulance," Brian stated, feeling his limp hand. "He has no pulse."

There was no resuscitating Peter Townsend. He had breathed his last breath. He couldn't shake the depression and he drank himself into alcohol poisoning. The coroner had never seen a case with such a high blood alcohol content.

Peter had drifted out of his body and was enjoying the float around his town when he saw the darting shadows. He hoped they wouldn't spot him, and he drifted behind the massive elm tree by the town square where the townspeople years before had hung a Torrey traitor and left him until crows had nearly picked his bones white. He knew he was dead, but he rather enjoyed being out of his body, free from worry. . . .

Octonoo, a massive serpent-like being with eight arms, saw him and sang to him, "Peter, it's your time."

From a distance, Octonoo was enchanting, wraith-like. He still sported the silver and gold garments that he had grown accustomed to while serving in the Circle of Light. As he grew closer, Peter could make out his razor-sharp teeth and bluish eyes. He found himself being bound with chains and dragged about town.

"It will be your last view, Peter. Where you're going, there's no return," Octonoo chanted.

"But why can't I stay here?" Peter implored. "I have family here, a house, a business."

"I know," Octonoo said empathetically. "It's sad, isn't it, to leave it all behind. You've gathered your riches for others to spend. But the one treasure that you should have found you forsook. Now you are ours for all eternity."

Santero wanted to meet Peter before he was thrown into the Lake of Fire. He was curious why such powerful guardians were sent to watch over his daughter and her boyfriend. He chose to interrogate Peter personally and learn what he could.

The room was black, but Peter could feel the presence all around him. The fallen had grown accustomed to living in the outer darkness and rather preferred it. Peter hadn't. It was unbearably terrifying.

"You know who I am, don't you?" Santero bellowed. "I am the Lord of the Night. You are in my domain until I rise to overthrow the Mighty One and his guardians. Your stay shall be a long and unpleasant one. To begin with, there are some things I need to know. Tell me what you know of this Brian Phillips," Santero commanded.

"I only met him once." Peter cowered back as far from the voice as he could get. "My daughter said he was brilliant, that he made a dead lobster come to life."

"Surely there are other things you know that you are not telling us. The Mighty One has assigned guardians to protect him and your daughter. Surely you know their plans. It is most unusual for a guardian the stature of Raphael to guard ones so young." Santero roared, "You will tell me."

Peter gasped as he saw Santero's face in full rage. His teeth were sharpened like stiletto's breath as foul as sulphur. Peter was lifted up by the neck.

"Must I reduce you to a pile of cinders for you to disclose what their plans were?"

"Wait," Peter said, nearly choking, "I know they are planning on attending Stanford. Brian got a full scholarship.

I know Alice is planning on visiting him and attending there as well. Really, that's all I know."

"To the Lake with you!" Santero pitched him far out of sight.

Santero turned to Cadaver. "It's time to double up the surveillance of Brian Phillips. We may yet thwart the Mighty One's plans for his life."

CHAPTER SEVEN

THE GIFT

Alice hadn't realized how wealthy her trust was until the lawyer sat her down and read her the will. Even though Harriet had run off, her father had never removed her from his will. She was amply provided for for the rest of her life. Alice's fortune was so diversified that the lawyer had logged over 20 hours just finding out the full value of it. After he was finished, he calculated it to be in the neighborhood of 25 million dollars. Her father had made provision for another trustee to be appointed until it was turned over to her at age 18, nine months away. She was astounded.

"Brian," Alice said, returning from the lawyer's office, "thanks for staying and helping us with the funeral arrangements. I don't know if I would have survived this without you. I don't think you'll ever realize just how much you mean to me. Brian, I know you're not going to be 17 until you've already started college, but I'd like you to know if you want me, I'd like to marry you."

Brian looked at her with a puzzled look. "Is this a proposal?"

"Yes, I suppose it is."

"I love you enough to marry you, Alice," Brian stated, twisting the ring on his index finger that she had given him there last summer on the Vineyard. "But how do you propose we support each other?"

"That's the great news," Alice beamed. "I just got back from Bert Yancy's office, my father's lawyer. I'm a millionaire. Not just one million, though, twenty-five jillion." She wrapped her arms around him. "I want to marry you to finance your dreams and raise a family together."

"Okay," Brian responded astonishingly, "I'm up for it. I accept. Let me at least get you a ring, though."

Brian's parents weren't too thrilled with the idea. They came up the next day to meet Alice's stepmom and talk about details. Massachusetts's law prohibited marriages under the age of 18 although New Hampshire was more lax. It required the parents' signatures on the documents. They arranged for Brian to miss a week of school.

The ceremony was short and simple. Only 40 people were there, a few of Brian's parents' best friends and some of Alice's schoolmates and neighbors, and a few of the regulars from the Wise Owl. Reverend Jacobs had checked into rehabilitation in Washington D.C. at Hope Hospital. He had arranged for an old Bible School chum, Tommy Van Horn, to come up and officiate.

The Seagram estate was repainted and flowers were planted everywhere. It never looked so beautiful. Alice and Brian had decided to keep it as their summer home and to allow her stepmom to remain there as long as she liked. A horse-drawn carriage pulled them up to the front door.

Brian's parents bought them tickets to Bermuda and hotel accommodations for an entire week. They left the reception to drive to Logan Airport where they spent the night at the airport hotel and left early for Bermuda the following day.

After they returned from a week of swimming, making love, dining, scuba diving, sailing, and general sightseeing, Alice moved in with the Phillips, who had replaced Brian's single bed with a hand-wrought iron poster bed. They repainted his room and put up some tasteful art prints. If it weren't for the fact that Brian was graduating at the top of his class and was to give the commencement speech, he would have never gone back to school.

When Brian walked down the hall at John Adams High located on Beacon Street, the girls who had ignored him for years wondered who he was. A handsome guy with a tan and a red Dodge Stealth. When they all found out he was the computer whiz and captain of the debating team, the next debate was full of single 16-year-olds with heart throbs. They were shocked to find out he was married and jealous when they saw Alice.

Tannersly Toys, the company started by Mia Tannersly's father, was a sponsor of the National Science Debate held every May in the Centennial Hall in downtown Washington D.C. The team from John Adams High had unanimously been selected to represent Massachusetts for the regional debates. Although the purpose was to generate an interest in science and inventiveness, Tannersly knew that the only people who could design truly innovational toys were those who loved to use them.

Tannersly, in years previous, had introduced the "furball." It could be twisted into any shape, size, or configuration, could bounce over houses, float in water, be used on tennis courts, baseball diamonds, racquetball courts, or simply bounced off walls. It was the most popular toy in North American, and that meant the world. The most amazing thing about the furball was that the hair was as soft and fine as a newborn baby and it never wore out. In fact, over time it would even grow. A patented genetic substance enabled the follicles on the furball to grow. Kids loved to shave them and watch the hair grow back. They loved to dye the hair with wild colors and cut it into mohawks. They weren't cheap, either. The list price was $39.95, but to the millions of children who had them, they were worth every penny. More than a couple of wealthy kids from the suburbs were set upon by mini bike and skateboard riding ghetto gangs who ripped off their backpacks and stole their furballs. Kids would literally kill for furballs and Tannersly knew it.

Even though they had massive success with the furball, the marketing people knew the future was in interactive video and computer toys. They were looking for someone gifted enough to develop their line and carry them into the 21st century.

Under Santero's orders, Marmorphis, a being who resembled a preying mantis with his misshapen wings and an elongated neck covered with boils, made continual suggestions to Mia Tannersly, the chairman, until she was relentlessly driven to start a new line of games that would give the fallen access to reprogram the minds of the children of the world. The purpose of the fallen was to so inundate the children with misleading information of the mystic and supernatural that they would be too confused to be able to separate wrong from right. They knew that if they could get the young children to be angry and violent, that the love of the Mighty One which alone had universal power to change the world for good would be thwarted.

Mia funded a special research project by the Darrow Neurological Research Center that tested heart rates, breathing patterns, and was able to predict increases of stress. She had designed a child's hand-held computer where the child would wear computer glasses with sensors that read the pulse from the child's temple. There were also small rubber receptacles that the children were instructed to place on their chests that would monitor breathing response, allowing the child to interact with the computer. It worked beautifully. Their only problem was finding a programmer to design the appropriate games. Until she had the right design and application, she was reluctant to unveil her discovery. She knew it would be worth mega bucks and gross, perhaps billions of dollars.

* * * * *

The Circle of Light hummed with activity. Because of the great number of abortions taking place on the planet and the thousands of children dying daily of starvation, new souls were being added as fast as the guardians could bring them up. As soon as they were brought up, they were shown through the Celestial City. They knew the Mighty One as their Creator and as the one who loved them. They had not made a conscious decision to follow him, but each one was received as if they had followed him for a long life.

Trish never got a chance to live her life. She was to have been a microbiologist. It was the Mighty One's plan that after graduate school she would discover gene splicing for cancer patients, thus forever eliminating cancer as a life-threatening disease. Her mother, Patricia Underwood, worked for Pan American Airlines right up until it went out of business. At age 28 she became pregnant and decided it would be better to have an abortion than to raise a child while she was still unmarried and unsure about her livelihood. The abortionist had been kind to her, and after it was over and baby Trish had been hacked to pieces inside her womb, she felt an immense sorrow. Little did she know of the Mighty One's plans to bring her a husband and use her daughter in such a great way. She turned back to the Mighty One out of grief and for forgiveness, but for Trish there was to be no life on earth, no flowers to smell, strawberries to taste, or young boys to write poems to. No puzzles to solve, mysteries to unlock, or diseases to help cure. Life was over for her even before it began. Although the Mighty One enjoyed the newlings, as they called them, he yearned for His Kingdom to reign on earth as it did in Heaven. In His infinite wisdom, He gave the gift to another who would grow up in another part of the planet and hopefully use her talents to solve one of life's most devastating mysteries.

Santero entered, hoping to evoke fear. No one cowered from him. They knew he had come purposely to find out what the Mighty One was up to.

"Have you seen my servant, Brian Phillips, Santero?" the Mighty One beamed. "Immense wisdom for one so young."

"Yes, immense and deep and a fortune to back it up with. Haven't you made his path just a little too easy? He gets the girl and the money. Who wouldn't follow you on earth for those benefits? What about the way of hardship?" Santero queried.

"What interest do you have in the chosen, learning their faith through hardship? Brian serves me out of love and he has applied his wisdom to learn My word. It is the reason your servants can't touch him," the Mighty One thundered.

"Can't touch him indeed. You have assigned no less than one of your great commanders to guard him, Raphael and Uzziah, who offered up Your sacrifices. Remove them from guarding him and see if he can stand on his own with just his knowledge of Bible verses. I say he is not standing on his own, but rather being delivered from temptations before he has even seen them. Let me tempt him and test him. Do you really think he'll come through?" Santero gloated.

"Very well, I'll remove Uzziah and Raphael from guiding him, but I'll not permit you to harm even one hair on his head. Go now, your presence saddens me, O Star of the Morning, you who I created. Now you enjoy nothing but a tormentor," the Mighty One spoke, standing in the throne.

"Are you saying you made a mistake?" Santero taunted.

"Giving you the power of choice was necessary, Santero," the Mighty One retorted. "It wasn't a mistake on my part. The mistake occurred when you railed against the One who made you and you mistook My glory and My majesty for your own. Look at you now. You are but a shadow of what you were. A shadow without light, without substance. I am love. My kingdom is a kingdom of love, not force. I shall not force anyone to accept my love or my rule. I give to all the same choice I gave to you and to the guardians who chose to remain with me even after you enticed them with lies to rebel against me. I only wish that your spirit had not turned. You know power and you know suffering and you know pain. Yet, with all this knowledge, you have no joy. You are emptier now than before you had this knowledge. You have become a god but not one who loves and creates, one who hates and destroys. You forget one thing, Santero. I live in eternity, not in the realm of time which you live in. I know all things that were, that are, and that are to be. I know whatever you give Brian Phillips to make him follow your path will ultimately fail. Nothing can take him out of my hands. We have engraved him on the palms of our hands. We have suffered death for his transgressions and shall forever enjoy the pleasure of his worship. How I wish that you had never left, that somehow you had made the right choice when you were drawn up with pride, but you didn't. It is sad, but for you there is no hope."

"Save your speeches, Mighty One. I need not love. I see it as a degenerative weakness, not a strength. I care not for what reasons my followers obey me, only that they do so unquestionably. I care not for their mental ascent, just their blind obedience. I desire them to be my slaves to do my bidding, for I intend to see you cast down to the very Hell that You created for me and the other fallen. Perhaps Your great omnipotent mind blocks out what Your end will be. Or is it that You just can't admit to Your mistakes? Look at Your followers. They are weak, they are few. They spend little time talking with You. On Your Holy Days, it is more likely to find them occupied with vacationing, boating, golfing, shopping, watching sporting events, and even sleeping. And at best they are but a fraction of the population. Many, many more follow me under the guise of many truths. Who is the wiser, Mighty One? Even those who claim to belong to You follow me in murdering their young, in withdrawing away from the needs of their unfortunate brethren. How many Mother Theresas do You have, Mighty One, that have forsaken all to follow You? You have many more that serve You and are rich in the things of the world. Would they serve You with nothing, as my adherents do in India, even refusing to eat the animals that would bring them life? Would they put themselves in danger to further your cause as my Shiites do, who gladly lay down their lives for an Allah that does not even exist? Do they even give one year or two years to serve Your great commission while my false prophets go door-to-door without charge, winning people to the words of Joseph Smith, copied from a science fiction book. I think not. Yes, I shall leave Your accused presence, but at least keep Your word and withdraw your messengers from Brian Phillips."

Santero vanished in a cloud of black smoke.

Alice decided that finishing high school was not a priority. She opted to study for her GED certificate and not go back to Shipley. She found life at Brian's most pleasant and enjoyed being around his mom and dad and learning more about him—things that she knew would prepare her to be a good wife. The staggering amount of money she received didn't make sense to her until tax time when she learned that her estate had made nearly 1.7 million dollars that year just from investments.

"Hi, Brian," she said as he returned from high school. "You ready to go to Washington?"

"Yeah, you've never been there, have you?" Brian asked.

"No, my dad never likes to leave his business with anyone, and my aunt and uncle, well, they're just holed up on the Vineyard every summer. I'd like to go to the Smithsonian, though. Do you think it would be possible?" Alice wondered.

"Yeah, what are those forms?" he pointed.

"My taxes. Do you know that the estate made 1.7 million last year? My tax bill is almost 800 thousand dollars. It's a lot of money. We really should start funding some of your experiments. Why don't you bring Louie to the debate? Maybe some people would like him."

"You really think I should bring Louie?" Brian hinted. "I mean, this isn't a science fair."

"The debate's on artificial intelligence, right?"

"Yeah," Brian answered.

"Well, isn't Louie artificial intelligence?"

"Yeah, I guess you're right. I'll put him in one of those pet carry-ons."

The airport security didn't know what to make of Brian's pet lobster, but they were busy with commuter flights and waved him through. They landed at Dulles and took the Metro in to Washington where they had been booked into the Sheraton. They were greeted by an oriental woman wearing a red linen jacket carrying a clipboard.

"Are you here for the debate?" she inquired.

"Yes, Brian Phillips from John Adams, Boston. This is my wife, Alice Phillips," Brian beamed.

"Well, quite young to be married. Let me see, you have been preregistered. They have you in room 1967. You should get quite a good view of the capitol. I don't know if the hotel will allow you to keep pets, though," she added.

"It's not alive. It's a robot I made."

Brian and Alice checked into the room. Brian could feel that something was different. He felt restless and couldn't quite explain it. He chalked it up to unfamiliar surroundings and decided to make the best of it. After flopping on the bed and switching through the channels on cable, he turned his attention to the capitol.

"Can you believe it? Here we are married and I'm not even old enough to vote."

Alice hugged him. "You're still old enough to be a great husband. Did I ever tell you that was the best honeymoon I ever had?" she joked.

"No, you didn't." He grabbed her. "Just how many honeymoons have you been on?"

"Stop." He began tickling her. "I told you no."

They began tickling each other and ended up late for the evening meal. When they did go down, they found their places set and everyone from his high school looked at him coyly.

From the front of the banquet room, the beautiful oriental Mia Tannersly addressed the gathering.

"You are all the future leaders of this great country. America has always been on the forefront of innovation and design. Imagination is what rules the world. It is those who dream who make their dreams a reality for the rest of mankind. We have chosen to sponsor this contest with the hopes that some of you will choose careers in design and make our earth a better place to live. In mainland China, over one billion people live. Many exist in poverty while surrounded by wealth. I wish that all would be able to enjoy the bounty from the earth. It is truly plenteous. To the team that wins, we will be donating 50 thousand dollars of the latest computer-aided design equipment. It will truly be of benefit to their school. We want to welcome you. You represent the best America has to offer. This evening there are several things arranged for you. The Kennedy Center is hosting a special performance by Leonard Bernstein. Or if you wish, we have made special arrangements for the National Museum of Science to give us an after-hours tour. Enjoy yourselves and welcome to Washington D.C."

"Alice, can you believe it? The National Museum of Science," Brian beamed. "You want to go or hear Leonard Bernstein?"

"Let's do the museum," Alice noted. "Doesn't she seem awfully young to head up a multi-international company like Tannersly Products? There is something very strange about her."

"Well, she probably is young but you're a multi-millionaire and you're young as well."

They finished the cheesecake set before them on the table and approached the speaker's podium where Mia was addressing the girl who greeted them.

"Excuse me," Brian spoke, "we're, or rather I'm from John Adams High. I'd like to get an extra pass to the science museum for my wife, Alice. We got married just recently."

Mia studied him intensely and she looked at her assistant. "Lusa, will you arrange for a pass for this young man's wife?" She stuck out her hand. "I'm Mia Tannersly."

Alice accepted her handshake. She looked her in the eyes and noticed the absence of light.

"Alice Phillips," she responded. "We invested in your company years ago. We made quite a fortune."

"Thank you," Mia said, turning away differentially.

"How is your pet lobster?" Lusa spoke. "He must be pleased to have not been on the menu."

"Louie is fine," Brian spoke. "Yes, if you'd like to see more of him, I could arrange it."

"A pet lobster?" Mia was puzzled. "You've brought a pet lobster with you?"

"A mere example of my own creation of a walking, talking, sensing, seeing miniature robot. He speaks seven languages and can answer over 100,000 questions," Brian spoke proudly.

"Well," Mia made a mental note, "Brian Phillips, I look forward to seeing your debate. Usually it's frowned upon to bring things to them, but I must admit you have my curiosity. She will assist you with an additional pass. You must excuse me, it's daybreak in the Far East and we are building a new factory. Unfortunately it has not been without its problems."

Marmorphis spoke to her subconscious. "Don't let this one get away. A pet lobster. This could be the young person you're looking for. The next wave."

As Mia stepped out of the banquet room, she took a quick glance back at Brian. Her eyes met Alice's and she sensed a conflict.

Although Raphael and Uzziah had been withdrawn as Brian's guardian, Ballelulia was still very much on duty. Through the constant prayer of the young married couple, his power had grown more and more.

"You seek to destroy these young ones, do you not Marmorphis?" Ballelulia asked.

"Ask your all-knowing Mighty One," Marmorphis countered. "Don't bother me. You feel all high and mighty. One day this Kingdom of Love that you stand on will become as weak as the shifting sands. The earth and its people have been given to us by their ancestors Adam and Eve. You are the trespasser here."

"No, you have it wrong, Marmorphis. The earth is the Lord's and everything therein. Those who serve you shall only meet the same end as you. Now please step out of my way. We have places to go, where I'm sure you would not enjoy yourself."

"Brian," Alice spoke, "I was talking to my mom and she said if I could, maybe I should visit Reverend Jacobs in Hope Care Center. I checked while you were taking a shower. They have a service tonight in about 45 minutes. Do you think we could go over? I'm not even a little tired."

"Yeah," Brian said enthusiastically, "it probably would do him good having a visitor. You sure we can get in?"

"Yeah," Alice said shrugging her shoulders. "I felt strange around that Chinese girl, didn't you? Like a cold draft?"

"No, I didn't really feel anything strange. She seemed pretty nice. Let's go. I don't want to be up all night. I want to go over some of my notes for the debates. After all, that's why I'm here," Brian said as he pulled Alice's arm.

"Well, lover boy," Alice beamed, "that isn't why I'm here. I'm here to keep you warm at night and make sure none of these girls get their hands on you."

Hope Care Center was located on the outskirts of the beltway. Developed by an ex-cocaine dealer, its primary purpose was to help people stop their self-destructive behavior patterns. As a minister, Reverend Jacobs had been provided with an adequate group medical insurance plan. They paid the $1,200 per day for round-the-clock care, hospitalization, and therapy by the country's best. The cure rate was nothing short of miraculous. The furnishings were unassuming: very home like with several antique couches, subdued lighting, and old oriental rugs. Brian and Alice were warmly greeted by a matronly woman, rather stout, with a slight German accent.

"Gut evening," the nurse spoke, "how may I help you two?"

"Well, I was told we could come and see Reverend Jacobs," Alice spoke. "I'm from New Hampshire. We're in town and he used to be the pastor of my church."

"Let's see Reverend Jacobs. Oh," the nurse laughed, "I never would have thought Rich was a minister. He's a very funny man, always pulling some practical joke or another. Go right in. They're having their evening get together. Down the hall, second door on the right."

The meeting was intense when Alice and Brian slipped in the door. They took seats in the back row and watched as Blain Atchinson poured out her heart telling about her first drink at age 13. She went on tell about her frequent blackouts in high school and how she didn't even remember her wedding night. Most of her life was a big blank.

"I think you need to face your life, Blain," Rich spoke. "You can't hide by just getting drunk all day long. There are times that things are hard and painful. It's just part of life, but there's also times when things are great. If you're drunk, you'll miss it all."

Alice nudged Brian and whispered, "He looks great, doesn't he?"

Brian nodded in agreement.

The therapist, wearing a tweed sports coat with leather patches on the arms and fairly thick, black, horn-rimmed glasses, stood up. "How many here feel that Blain has missed a significant portion of her life?"

The crowd all raised their hands.

"Blain, none of your friends here think what you are doing is healthy. You still have a whole life ahead of you if you want it. You have to learn to cast your cares on Christ not to shoulder them yourself or to put them at the bottom of a bottle. I want everyone here to close their eyes. Now visualize with me. You are carrying a big sack of potatoes slung over your shoulder. It's heavy, it's weighing you down. Now look at those potatoes. One is labeled 'Rejection, what do people think of me?' One is labeled 'Will anyone really love me if they know who I am?' One is labeled 'Home, where will I live?' Take those cares now and lay them down in front of you. Now visualize Jesus, only He's much bigger than you imagine Him. His hand is as wide as a swimming pool. You see His hand. It is reaching down and taking your cares. He's removing them from in front of you. They belong to Him. Leave them there. Have no thought for tomorrow, just take care of today. Today is fine. God is on the throne. He reigns."

The people went up to the front and embraced Blain. She wiped the tears away from her eyes. Brian and Alice went up to Rich, who was talking with her.

"Reverend Jacobs," Alice said.

Rich looked around, surprised to see them. "Alice and Brian, what on earth brings you down to Washington?"

"I'm in town for a debating contest," Brian said. "You know, we're married." Brian showed off his marriage ring.

"Look, Alice, I know what happened didn't help out your father's condition and probably contributed to his death," Rich spoke sincerely.

"But it was . . ." Alice began to say.

"I know you can tell me it wasn't my fault, but I'm here and I'm learning to admit to responsibility for things I'm responsible for. I caused your mom to leave him and caused your parents a lot of suffering all while being a man of the cloth. I abused my position of trust to the entire community. I don't know if God will ever let me make it up, but I'm going to spend the rest of my life trying. You tell your mom I'm still praying for her. You tell your mom I'm sorry for what I did to her and that I love her and maybe someday God will give me the chance to . . ."

"Reverend Jacobs," Brian interjected, "we didn't come to hear your apology. We know that you were duped as well by another power. We came to let you know there are no hard feelings."

"Brian, before I fell, God gave me a prophetic gift. The Lord has a word for you that you need to heed. The time is coming when your gift shall be sought after for 'purposes outside of My will,' saith the Lord. 'Do not heed to other voices, but heed only to mine.'"

"What does that mean?" Brian asked. "Other voices? What kind of voices?"

"There is the voice of the Mighty One," Reverend Jacobs counseled. "And there are other voices, from the myriads of the fallen who would tickle your ears with vain, glorious promises and pride, appealing to every dark secret within you. Heed it, Brian. If you follow His voice, you'll never go astray."

The taxi ride back to the hotel was long and slow. Brian wished he had his car to speed through what little traffic there was going back into the city, although there seemed to be a steady stream coming out from the city. Alice was immersed in her own thoughts when Brian tapped her on the shoulder.

"What did you think of what he had to say to me?" Brian asked. "To be honest, I don't know what to make of it. I know it talks about prophecies in the Bible. But that was then, this is now."

"I think you should just be careful about what you do with your talents. You're a genius, Brian. There are not many like you in the world. The Evil One would like nothing better than for you to get sucked into something ignorantly to divert your talent from Good to Evil."

The hall was packed with parents, educators, and observers as the debate teams assembled. John Adams High advanced automatically to the semi-finals because of their undefeated record in East Coast schools. They were debating St. Ignatious High School from Cleveland, Ohio, captained by Derek Sweeney, the son of a well-known democratic congressman.

"Will the team captains please step to the podium," the moderator spoke.

Brian and Derek advanced to the front where they exchanged handshakes and smiles. They were handed envelopes.

"The issue is, 'Will the high tech revolution replace most jobs leading American society down the road to a society run by computers?'" the moderator spoke. "You may open your envelopes and read what side you have been chosen to argue." The captains opened their envelopes. "Please read out loud."

Brian spoke, "Our team has been chosen to argue in opposition to this point."

Derek said, "Our team has been chosen to support this position."

"Very well, the envelopes having been opened, each of you captains may pick your team members to support your points. Positions and rebuttals shall be clocked and are not allowed to be over five minutes in length. The team from St. Ignatious shall give the final rebuttal. Are the rules clear?"

After two grueling days of debates, the excitement was at high zenith for the semi-finals. Brian looked from his table and received an encouraging smile from Alice. His team smartly presented their arguments for high tech, the increased amount of society management, the freeing of personal time for the pursuit of living, the fact that it was here and in use, and society could be built around it if it were properly implemented. The team from St. Ignatious took a fairly ordinary tact in rebuttals, inhumanization of the workplace, people being unemployed as jobs were taken over by robots, and the general wasting of the human mind. Brian stood to present the final point.

"In all deference to my esteemed opponents from Ohio," Brian addressed the assembly, "high tech is here to stay. No company that has automated has decided to regress. No company that has properly implemented the use of computers for laborious and repetitive tasks has decided to go back to the old ways of bookkeeping or design. As our society has grown more and more complex, we have developed a symbiotic relationship with computers. They are everywhere. Interactive videos and golf for home amusement, data spreadsheets for instant on-the-job cost quotations, information at the touch of a button. Language interpreters enable us to communicate with everyone, expanding business from local and national to global in scope. I am looking forward to a career in computer design. Before I met my wife, my best friend was a computer." Brian pulled out Louie and allowed him to walk on the table in front of him. "Louie, good morning. Are you enjoying Washington D.C.?"

"I'd like it better if you wouldn't keep me in that stuffy old shoe box. Haven't you ever heard of odor eaters?" Louie cracked.

The crowd went into shock and hysterics.

"Sure, I've heard of them, Louie. I didn't know your sense of smell was that developed," Brian quipped.

Louie turned and looked in Brian's direction. "Well, I can smell a faint linger of perfume on you and it doesn't smell like anything your wife Alice wears."

The audience went out of control.

"Well," Brian answered, "maybe it's time to put you back in the box." Brian lifted Louie up to put him back in the box.

"No, please," Louie pleaded, "I promise I'll be good."

Brian turned Louie off and placed him back under his table. He gathered his composure while glancing around the room for approval. His chest burst with pride. He had unveiled his invention, and it was a rousing success. "To close my point," Brian addressed, "computers need not be inhuman, sterile. They are an image of their creators, even as we are made in the image of our Creator and bear His likeness. Thank you."

The applause was deafening and unrelenting. Mia turned to her assistant. "Offer him anything," Mia spoke. "I want him for our company. I don't care what it costs or what you have to do to get him, Lusa. Do you understand?"

"Yes, Miss Tannersly," Lusa answered, "we'll have him."

CHAPTER EIGHT

THE TRAP

Marmorphis entered the cave to meet with Santero for further commands. He was growing more and more uncomfortable below ground and thoroughly enjoyed being inside Mia Tannersly. It wasn't just the freedom of roaming about on the planet. It was his ability to control someone else's will totally, to make suggestions and see them followed with such clarity of purpose. He resented Santero telling him what to do. He had long lost belief in Santero's divinity and knew that besides the power that Santero had gathered for himself, there was nothing at all different about them. It was hard to show any respect for one whom he had witnessed making countless mistakes.

"Your greatness," Marmorphis bowed in feigned subservience, "your plan seems to be going well. Mia has already made inquiries for the price of Brian Phillips' soul. Hopefully it won't come at too great a cost."

"Very witty indeed, Marmorphis," Santero grunted. "The poor humans don't even know the value of their blasted eternal souls. Most sell them for mere pennies. Their stupidity never ceases to amaze me. The teaming masses under the Shou Lin Temple are ready to once again enter the world. I want you to make absolutely sure that the factory is complete—no more delays. Why have you not created enmity between the Phillips? Newlyweds always have arguments."

"It's impossible. She prays for him all the time, and Ballelulia has grown bold in the defense of both of them."

"Drat, the Mighty One fooled me. I bargained him into removing Uzziah and Raphael after the two were joined in marriage, but Ballelulia guards him as well when they are together." Santero towered over Marmorphis, his eyes a crimson red. "Make sure she doesn't join him when he visits

Tannersly Industries. Do something to keep them separated—anything. Don't fail, Marmorphis. Our lake awaits those who fail and I know that you fancy your freedom."

"I shan't fail, Oh Great One. I shall bring them apart."

* * * * *

"Alice, have you seen my razor?" Brian asked. "Darn, it was my last blade. Why can't you get your own to shave your legs?"

Alice poked her head out of the shower. "I'm just keeping my legs smooth for you. You can go down to the lobby. They sell razors."

"There's hardly time. The lady from Tannersly Industries wants to meet me in like 10 minutes," Brian answered.

"Well, then don't shave, Brian," Alice quipped. "Your beard isn't that heavy anyway. It's not like she's going to even notice and wear your blue suit. It makes you look older."

Brian walked out of the bathroom in a huff. He was beginning to wonder if he'd married too young after all. He stood in the hallway glancing up at the elevator. It seemed to take forever. Being on the 19th floor didn't help at all. By the time it finally arrived, Brian was convinced that Alice was beginning to be a bit of a chain around his neck. He still loved her, but he didn't want to carry her his whole life. When the door opened, he determined to make the most of his meeting with Tannersly Industries and not to be financially dependent on the inherited wealth of his wife. He decided whatever it took he would do.

Brian browsed through the hotel gift shop, bought himself some M&M's Peanuts, and started reading about the local tourist attractions. He watched the elevator door for

Alice. She exited and he walked over to her. He was still upset with her.

"Thanks, Alice, the meeting was supposed to be 10 minutes ago," Brian said, looking at his watch. "This is my big chance."

"I'm sorry," Alice said, shrugging her shoulders. "Would you rather just go without me?"

"No, I wouldn't rather go without you. I just wish you'd be on time," Brian said sharply as he grabbed her hand. "Let's just go. Talking about it isn't going to make it any easier."

They arrived at the restaurant just as Mia Tannersly and Lusa were arriving.

"Brian Phillips," Lusa spoke, "this is Mia Tannersly. You met the other day."

"Yes," Brian said, extending his hand. "You remember my wife, Alice?"

Mia extended her hand. "Yes, I do. That's a lovely dress you're wearing, very elegant. You must be very proud of your husband. He was sensational in his debate."

Yes," Lusa commented, "I will be surprised if your team does not win."

The waiter stepped to the front to show them to their seats. The restaurant was old money, Washington D.C. All of the furnishings were Sheraton style with pale blue carpeting and large, billowy draperies. The tables were impeccably set with pink linens and real silver and crystal. Brian felt his feet immerse in the thick carpeting. He looked around at the myriads of people having their power lunches. His chest swelled out with pride as he realized how lucky he was to have been discovered.

The waiter came, poured them all water, and brought them fresh croissants and butter. They were given menus and slowly made their decisions, commenting to each other on what would be the best choices. Brian and Lusa joked about the lobster salad and decided to order it anyway, Mia decided on the Dover sole cooked in lime butter, and Alice decided to have the small petite filet with the new potatoes. They all had the Caesar salad, the house specialty.

As they sampled the croissants and waited for their meal to arrive, Mia opened her attache case and pulled out some drawings.

"We've been combing the college campuses, toy firms, everywhere we could think of to find a designer who could program our new line. Tannersly Industries wants to move into mass manufacture of these Imps—every child's best friend." Mia pushed the drawings over so Brian could see them. As he looked, she continued, "We know you've been accepted for full scholarship at Stanford." She examined Brian's face for any reactions. "You don't suppose we didn't find out everything about you, did you? Anyway, Tannersly has offices in Palo Alto with quite an array of equipment. We'd like you to come work for us part-time. You'd have your own lab, assistants, and the ability to turn your inventions into reality."

Brian showed the drawings to Alice. "These things look sort of strange," Alice commented. "You said they were called the Imps. What exactly are they supposed to be?"

"They are very old mythological characters. Nearly every middle-aged culture had them. They dance, they sing. We want ours to be very much alive. We have been unable to find anyone with the imagination to make them truly come to life," Mia spoke.

"You want me to program these to dance and sing?" Brian asked.

The waiter brought over their food and they started eating their salads. Brian put the drawings aside.

"Movement for robotics is still a long way from being smooth. I've seen Barishnicov perform, but having a machine dance like that while singing?" Brian wondered. "I mean, technically it could be done. We have sophisticated enough chips and the hardware is in place, but the software would have to be developed. When did you want to introduce these and start marketing them?"

"You're not thinking of this seriously, Brian. Don't you think we should talk about it? Is that what you want to use your gift for, developing toys?" Alice questioned, trying to keep her composure.

"Why not?" Brian retorted. "We'll be in Palo Alto. Computer Information is my major, and what I did with Louie is unique. It would certainly be a challenge, but why not? Miss Tannersly, what sort of compensation are we talking about?"

"Well, to begin with, any design you come up with to actually make these work, we would give you an industry standard eight percent royalty on all sales worldwide as well as, say 10 thousand a month." She smiled. "How does that sound?"

Brian put down his fork and slid his chair back. "I can't make this type of decision on my own. Would you mind if I just stepped out in the lobby for a short conference with my wife? This really has to be both of our decision or it won't work."

"Yes, be our guests. Take some time. I'll tell the waiter to hold the main course until you return."

Alice got up and followed him into the hall. They sat in front of the bay window in two Chippendale wing-backs overlooking a huge flower garden.

"I think this is too hasty. It just doesn't feel right. It's the first offer and you're going to find yourself tied up for life," Alice pleaded.

"Alice, I've always been my own person. No one is going to own me. I'm very good at what I do, and why shouldn't I benefit from my gift? It's the perfect opportunity. My own lab, Alice. It means you don't have to withdraw all of your inheritance. I can support you just like the Bible says." Brian touched her hand.

"So, Marmorphis," Ballelulia spoke, "you have laid your trap."

"What trap?" Marmorphis sneered. "My host has merely offered the boy a chance to use his gift. Doesn't the Mighty One speak of using your talents?"

"Yes, indeed he does, but I suspect that this item you have is not intended for good, but for evil."

"Oh Swineflesh Ballelulia, Santero has more interesting things up his sleeve than toys. We've got nearly every popular singer on the globe working for us, bringing millions upon millions to their damnation. Not only that, counterfeit religions have the vast majority of the world thinking that they are on their way to paradise when, in fact, they are in danger of eternal damnation."

"Regardless of the extent of your influence, I inform you now that I will be unwavering in protecting this one from your influence."

Marmorphis drew close to Ballelulia, blowing hot air into his face. "I don't want to ruffle your feathers any more, Ballelulia, but don't you think you're a bit late? Your man has already swallowed our bait—hook, line, and sinker. I say right now, we have him eating out of our hands."

Marmorphis disappeared in a cloud of smoke, leaving Ballelulia wondering if Brian and Alice really would be all right. He knew that as of late they had started to disagree and that their prayer time had diminished. He was feeling his own power being sapped. He decided to journey to the Circle of Light and make an appearance on their behalf.

The Circle of Light welcomed him with a warm, encompassing awe that swept his fears aside as if they were leaves in a hurricane. The Mighty Wind from the throne billowed his wings and brought him before the Mighty One.

"Welcome, Guardian Ballelulia," the Mighty One spoke. "It is good to see you and for you to be here."

"I am still on assignment, oh Mighty One," Ballelulia responded. His memories of the Mighty One diminished before the majestic presence. "I need assistance in my guardianship. Perhaps you could send someone to encourage the two I am guarding to spend more time in prayer and worship. I feel my power growing weaker, and it will only be a matter of time before I cannot prevent their being placed in bondage. Your will be done, oh Mighty One."

"You have grown to love these children of mine, have you not, Ballelulia?" the Mighty One gently inquired.

"Yes, I have. It is that love that has brought me here on their behalf."

"Very well, you shall find that when they go to California. I have already prepared for what you have asked.

CHAPTER NINE

THE WARNING

The Tannersly complex in Palo Alto was a sleek five-story building with one-way mirrors on front and a huge, bronze obelisk in the lobby. The area of town was known for high tech. The initials read TCC and gave no indication to the average passerby of the nature of the business inside. Since inception one year earlier, Tannersly had spent no less than 25 million dollars in developing the Imps. The Imps were to be everything that the Cabbage Patch dolls and Barbies had failed at being. They were to all look different and even have different names. They were to speak seven languages and be marketed worldwide. They would be programmed to pick up the mannerisms and speech patterns of their owners and learn to mimic them, becoming nearly carbon copies of their owners. No toy was ever conceived that would have such universal appeal. Mia had placed nearly her entire fortune on the success or failure of the Imps.

Brian drove by the complex Saturday afternoon after they arrived. He was impressed by the architecture, different from the New England style that he had grown up with. He had never seen the Pacific Ocean with its windswept trees clinging to the rocks that dangled out over the shoreline. It was a scene of indescribable beauty. He picked Alice up and they headed out to a quaint seafood restaurant. He was happy to pay for their meal with his American Express Gold Card, one of his many perks.

"You like it?" Brian asked, looking over the candlelight at Alice. "You know, I don't think you've ever looked so beautiful. I mean, do you feel better about being here now?"

"Yeah," Alice said, "I came across an ad for a little church not too far from where we live. Let's go. Let's start things out right. This is the divorce capital of the country. I don't want us to be statistics."

"Yeah," Brian smiled, "I'd like to go. What's the name?"

"Alliance Christian Church, over in San Mateo. So we won't be able to stay up all night."

"Then we'd better get home early." Brian held her hand and pulled her over for a warm embrace.

* * * * *

Bruce Wainright felt power surging through his veins. He was a young looking 30 year-old, energetic, and very passionate. He clutched his Bible as if it was the only life jacket on a sinking ship. He held it over his head. His eyes were bloodshot and sweat was beading off his forehead as lowered the Bible out over the congregation at Alliance Christian Church.

"It's right in here," he explained. "Every answer to every problem. You unemployed, underemployed, God has the answer. You've have marital problems, lonely? This book has the answer. You need something from Mighty-One—direction in your life. A goal, a purpose. You'll find it here. It's a road map through this journey called life. Scoffers have come and gone: nonbelievers, false prophets, kings, dictators, sorcerers, millionaires, and people who were too busy to take a look. The problem is they didn't see the cliff at the end of their road. They were on the wrong road of life. They were on the wide path to destruction; they weren't on the straight and narrow way. They didn't have their eyes on the Lord. They didn't have the light for their eyes and the path for their feet. They were stumbling in the darkness even at noonday. Friends, I stand before you today a changed man, a man with a purpose, a man with inexplicable joy. I'm single, I have no wife, no relatives. My mom and dad died while I was still in college. I'm an only child with no relatives, but I'm not alone. I've got a friend who is with me always. My earthly father didn't leave me any treasures. His life insurance barely covered burying him and my dear old mother, God rest her soul. No, my earthly father told me one thing. Whatever you're going to be, be the best you can be.

"How many here can honestly say they are doing their best to follow the Mighty One's ways for their lives? Are you using your time, your talents, your finances to glorify the Mighty One? We look at the big stars like Billy Memphis, Hollywood's Magic Man. Five million dollars a film and we say, 'Well, if I had his talent, I'd really do something for the Mighty One.'

"I ask you, what are you doing with the talents you have? When is the last time you told someone you loved them or were praying for them? When is the last time you asked the Mighty One for direction and then looked in here for the right road for your life? There is a way that seems right to a man. Brothers, sisters, it seems right. Oh yes, many things seem right. It seems right to take that job at the liquor store. It pays seven dollars an hour and you need the money, but are you being a fruitful servant working there? Oh yes, it seems right to turn your head while your son comes home with new sneakers after pushing dope. Oh sister, hear me, I'm talkin to you. If the shoe fits, don't go looking for a new pair. Put in on. God reads your mail. He knows all about it. Oh, it seems right to tell that government welfare lady you've got no man living with you when all he does is hide in the closet when they come over to inspect.

"Get out of the closet and get into the prayer closet with the Lord. Get on your face, humble yourself, ask Him for help. He won't turn you away. He is the waymaker. If you're stuck in a pit of depression, addicted to narcotics, tobacco, or alcohol, he is the deliverer. If you are lost in life with no goals or no hope, you're on a dead-end street without a sign, without a clue. Look in here. It has the answers for you. God is calling your name, sister. God is calling your name, brother. God is calling your name, children. Come down now."

The crowd at Alliance Christian Church began to pour down to the altar. Several came down on crutches. A lady came dragging her teenaged son. Several came with their unmarried live-ins.

From the rear of the old building, Brian and Alice watched the action at the Alliance Christian Church. Neither of them had ever seen anything like it.

"Do you want to go down front?" Alice asked. "We could use some prayer."

"Right now, in front of all these people?" Brian asked.

"Yeah, why not?" Alice pulled his sleeve. "Come on."

They walked to the front, down a long aisle of threadbare carpeting. When they stopped at the front, they were approached by a middle-aged woman in a business suit. She placed her hands on both of their heads.

"The Lord is showing me a trap door," she prophesied. "You are both standing on the edge. He wants you to know that wherever you go, He'll be with you. Though even if you walk through the valley of the shadow of death, He'll be with you. The Lord knows that you are young and you don't have the wisdom or experience, but in spite of decisions that you have made in error, not being able to discern the Lord's voice, He is going to be merciful to you and lead you through the valley. And yes, He will strengthen your marriage and He even knows you are with child and your son will be healthy."

The lady stepped back and looked at Brian and Alice. They looked up at her in shock.

"How did you know so much about us?" Brian asked.

"It is the spirit of the Lord that reveals what He wills to His servants, the prophets," she answered. "Take that prophecy and when things get hard, remind each other about it."

Brian looked carefully at the other cars to avoid hitting them as he pulled his sleek Dodge Stealth out of the parking lot and onto the side street, heading for the freeway.

"What did you think of the service?" Alice asked.

"Pretty wild," Brian said, smiling. "I didn't know church could be so much fun. That lady on stage really got down on that tambourine, didn't she?"

"How about that man who danced back and forth in front of the platform?" Pretty amazing. I'd like to go back," Alice responded.

"Then let's. It would be good to meet some Christians out here. I looked through the campus activity book and there's no Christian groups listed."

* * * * *

Mia was occupied with going back and forth from Hong Kong, San Francisco, and Mainland China, where she was supervising the plant. She arrived at the Tannersly complex and found Brian sitting alone at his terminal examining data on the Imp project.

"Good afternoon, Mr. Phillips," Mia said with a smile. "Is everything quite satisfactory with your work environment?"

Brian looked up from his programming. "Yes, I've never been treated better. In fact, I got my computer teacher to allow me to use this project as a fulfillment for my degree, so I guess I'm being paid to go to school."

"You know, we've been having problems with our factory. There have been so many accidents, it seems the Chinese don't care much about safety. There are no labor laws as there are here. People are expendable resources," Mia stated matter-of-factly.

"Yes, I guess with a population of two billion, people would be replaceable. I need to ask you something, Miss Tannersly. You brought me in for design work, but you've already built the prototypes, and most or nearly all of the programming has been done. It's sort of like bringing in someone to put in the bridges and overpasses after the roads are already laid down. It would be much simpler for me to rewrite and redo the design. I see many different ways to streamline and make this project really work. Are you familiar with computers?"

"No, not very much. Why?"

"I've already come up with a redesign. The less chips this has, the longer it will last and the more popular it will become. Instead of it becoming obsolete after a year, we could design it to do different things every year by offering new modules. Here on the back where you were going to have the battery pack, why not put in a removable module complete with a slightly more expensive lithium battery, and instead of redesigning the entire toy every year, we could keep the same design and just sell new modules."

"In other words, for the same toy, kids could buy different modules."

"Yes," Brian exclaimed, smiling. "Exactly, we keep the basic same external shells, make the interior out of the same material they use for joint replacement—valenium. We can work out the movement parameters, but we know that we can improve the other sensory movements as our access to technology improves. Just think, instead of a business investing in an expensive security system, they could buy one of these toys that could alert them to any movement or smoke. We could develop them to analyze voices, we could replace receptionists, and do away with so many of the mundane jobs of the world."

"Technology replacing boredom," Mia acknowledged. "I like it. Let me try to understand what you're really saying. You don't view this as just a toy, do you?"

"No, not that it's not a fabulous companion for a kid, but it has a much greater potential. We can train children to talk to these toys to prepare them for the computer world, but we can already enter this technology into the marketplace with motion sensors, smell detectors, voice wave identification programming, and shade analysis. A modern video camera does nothing but pick up an image. We've already developed the software that lets our Imp recognize from sight who he is talking to. Our software lets him respond to his owner or any number of people that the Imp is programmed to recognize. It's revolutionary. We have come up with a concept that has a much wider and universal application."

"Well, I'm sold. This is the first time I've ever talked to a computer whiz who was also a marketing genius. Do what you need to do. I'll schedule a meeting first thing tomorrow. How does your wife like it here in California?" Mia asked.

"She likes it great. We like where we're living and she's going part-time to Bible school."

"I haven't eaten. Would you like to join me for a bite? There's a great Chinese place around the block," Mia offered.

"Can I take a rain check?" Brian asked, checking his watch. "I'm already running a bit late."

"Sure, we'll do it at a later point. You have a lot of wisdom for your age. I hope your wife knows she's really lucky."

"She's not the only one who's lucky," Brian responded. "I'm lucky to have her as well. Would you like to come by and see our place? I'm sure Alice wouldn't mind you coming for a visit."

"I wouldn't want to be an imposition," Mia feigned.

"No, not at all." Brian reached for the phone. "I'll just give her a call. I'm sure she'll love it. We haven't had any company, and well, I've been the guinea pig for all her new recipes, and half the stuff I've never eaten before, so I don't know if it's prepared right or not."

"Alice," Brian said into the phone, "hey, would you mind if Mia Tannersly came by for dinner with us? We're sort of in the middle of discussing some changes and I thought it would be great if she could come by."

"It's fine with her," Brian said, placing the receiver down.

"I don't have my car here. Could I ride with you?" Mia asked.

"Yeah, I'll drop you off later."

Outside Mia studied his car. She rubbed her hand sensuously over the red paint. "This is beautiful—a Dodge Stealth!"

"It was my graduation present from my mom and dad. I love it. Let me show you how it handles."

Mia gripped her door handles as the Stealth snaked down the steep incline. It was more like a ride on the Matterhorn than an automobile ride. The stereo was blasting with "Going Through the Motions" by Michael W. Smith and Brian was relishing every rpm.

They pulled in front of the condo in Palo Alto and nearly hit a middle-aged man who was walking a dalmatian. Brian weakly smiled at him as if to apologize.

"Where'd you learn to drive?" Mia asked breathlessly. "You're like a madman."

"No sense having a fast car and being afraid of it," Brian quipped. "I have good hand and eye coordination, good depth perception, and this car can stop on a dime, so why not? Some people like rocking chairs. I like speed."

Ballelulia sensed the presence of the fallen Marmorphis miles before he came in the house with Mia. The air bristled with electricity as he challenged him at the door.

"You're not welcome here, Marmorphis," Ballelulia spoke with authority.

"Step aside, Guardian. I see no one here to bind me. Unless you wish your feathers to be in a state of disarray, I suggest you leave," Marmorphis taunted.

Ballelulia thought for a moment and knew that his charge had not bound the workers of iniquity the powers in dark places. He stepped back and allowed Marmorphis to pass.

"Won't you ever grow tired of toying with these humans?" Ballelulia asked, hoping to catch Marmorphis at a moment of weakness.

"Does a spider ever grow tired of playing with its victim, Ballelulia? I enjoy it." He smiled gleefully. "I find it quite amusing. When I find a place to dwell in one of these humans because they have opened the door in their spirit to me, I rather enjoy numbing them to life in general. I prefer making suggestions that will benefit my master, Santero."

"Even if it means their eventual destruction."

"So be it if it does. It is just your viewpoint, Ballelulia. How do you know the Mighty One will be triumphant? How do you know it is not to be Santero that will rule and reign forever?" Marmorphis drew his sword and sunk a barb into Ballelulia.

Mia looked about and stared straight at Alice.

"Indeed, who did your decorating? Quite quaint." She pointed to a bean bag chair. "I must say, it's been a while since I saw one of these. And these posters are quite a rage."

The comments made Alice feel inadequate. "I did," she answered, excusing herself. "I like sitting in bean bags watching T.V. and I love old movie posters. Some day I'm going to write a screenplay."

"Oh, and what is it you do now when your husband is at school or at work?" Mia taunted.

"I'm studying for my GED," Alice explained. "I got married before I graduated, so before I can enroll in college, I have to get a high school degree. And I'm taking bible school classes."

Mia looked at Brian with a show of pity as if he had befriended a mentally handicapped person. Brian saw the hurt on Alice's face and stepped to her side to bolster her self-confidence. "What's for dinner?"

"Well, I didn't have much time, so I thought we'd have roast chicken, a salad, and potatoes au gratin. It should be done in about 15 minutes."

"Great," Brian said, putting down his jacket. "I'm going to get changed. Why don't you two get to know each other a little better?"

"That was quite uncalled for, Marmorphis," Ballelulia chided. "A cheap shot at best, wounding my charge's self-esteem." Ballelulia drew out his sword and knocked the spike out of Marmorphis' hand. "Perhaps it's time for you to see real warfare."

"That's the loveliest silk dress I've ever seen, Ms. Tannersly," Alice smiled. "Come to think of it, every time I see you, I wish I knew as much about fashion as you do. Where I grew up, there wasn't much of a selection of clothes to pick from. We had a Wal-Mart and one local women's store, but it mostly catered to an older, conservative crowd. I took to wearing my dad's old shirts and cutoffs most of the time."

"You're a very lovely girl," Mia responded, sorry that she had insulted such an innocent person, and feeling a pang of guilt run through her heart as if shot with a javelin.

"Thank you," Alice smiled. She offered a tray of mushroom caps stuffed with crab. "Try one of these. It's an old family tradition."

Mia took one and bit into it. "It's delicious."

The dinner was lovely, and Mia commented several times on it. Alice beamed from the attention and Brian frequently smiled at her.

"You should be proud of Brian. He has discovered a whole new realm of possibilities to market our Imps."

"Removable microprocessors with individual programming in each. No one is exactly the same. They're all capable of voice, movement, and visual identification," Brian said.

"It's a wonderful idea." Mia suggested, "One certainly deserving of more than your present fee. I'll have my lawyer draw you up a larger profit-sharing plan."

"It's really not necessary," Brian interjected, looking proudly at Alice.

"Yes," Mia reflected, "it is. An inventor should always receive proper compensation for his invention."

Brian fell into the trap and reflected on how brilliant he had become. The seed of self-assurance planted itself deep in his heart.

* * * * *

Deep in the earth's core, Santero was monitoring the events. He knew his time had come to resurface and direct his next plan for the conquest of human hearts and souls. His thoughts of a mass reprogramming of human thought and belief patterns based out of Tannersly Products masterminded by an ignorant follower of the Mighty One made him smile.

"How much have you offered him?" Santero spoke to Marmorphis.

"She has given him 15 percent of the company," Marmorphis spoke. "He'll never even be able to think of ways to spend all of the money. Already he's out looking for some ocean-front property to build his own state-of-the-art fully computerized home. He's taken the bait."

"Nonetheless," Santero rose, "I have decided to intervene personally. I will be entering Wedge Harwood. See that nothing interferes."

The Circle of Light shined for all of the galaxies to see. From the black hole emerged the fallen one who had desired to rule over the Circle in place of the Mighty One. How he loathed having to ask the permission of the Mighty One for his every move. He disdained the Mighty One and hoped for the time when he could usurp the Kingdom of Light and drag his minions with him.

Archangel Michael stood before him, his sword a translucent steel with a razor-sharp edge. "You have come to visit us again, oh Fallen One," Michael thundered. "Don't you tire of toying with these humans?"

Santero stopped and looked at the one who had defeated him, casting him forever from his place alongside the throne. "I see you still keep your sword polished. Perhaps you will meet another worthy adversary, hardly one as worthy as myself. I don't tire of the humans. I may grow impatient thinking of new ways to destroy their wretched lives, but I'm not bored. It still rather amuses me. They're like ants running to and fro storing up their bits of food and gold and silver, not ever knowing when the foot will come down and crush their miserable necks. Ironic, isn't it? They struggle for that which they can never attain when the all-powerful Mighty One wishes to give them all things freely."

Michael stepped aside. "You may pass. The time when you shall be allowed to visit us has been shortened. There is only so much destruction that you shall be permitted. Only that which may be corrupted will be corrupted. Then we will bind you and yours and cast you into the lake where you so gleefully cast those who have blindly followed you."

Santero looked at him with fear and false pride. "Maybe not. I'm not the same one who battled you eons ago, Michael. I've learned some new tricks."

"You may have indeed, but there is one thing you should have learned from the creation that you have so successfully corrupted. Light always dispels darkness. It shines through the blackest cloud. You are in darkness and we walk in light. There will never be a place for your darkness to mingle with our light. If it was to be so, the Mighty One would have allowed you to remain. You have chosen your path even after you tasted the goodness of your Creator."

Santero looked surprised.

"Yes," Michael continued, "you may think you've been around so long that you had no beginning, that you existed eternally like the one you curse, but you are His creation, Santero. His creation you will always be. Only the Mighty One has no beginning and no end. Our only life lies in abiding in Him. You may pass."

Michael stood out of the way and allowed Santero to go into the Circle of Light.

The light was blinding to Santero. He was used to the fetid vapor that rose from the lake where he made his abode. He covered his eyes with his disfigured hand and approached the throne, trying to look majestic.

"What is it you wish with the children of men, Santero?" the Mighty One requested.

"We have a legion of small ones all entrapped under the old monastery. We wish to allow them to enter the bodies of a new computer toy so they may swarm about the earth." Santero paused, baiting the trap. "I have read in Your word where You gave the sons of men over to deceitful spirits even if it were possible to deceive the very elite. Surely as you had your servants' predict that it would happen, it is now time."

"I need not ask you what your purpose is, for I know that although you used to exist to bring glory and honor to my throne, you now only exist to bring it discredit. I don't need you to remind me that time is short, for the earth can barely contain the evil that is now practiced. I will allow you to bring out your fallen ones. I will withdraw my guardian who keeps them in their bonds, but the moment my followers cry out to me in repentance with tears for those that your fallen ones will torment, you know what will happen," the Mighty One replied.

"Your followers are weak. They don't even bother going to worship You on Sundays if it conflicts with a sports event or family outing," Santero retorted. "They neglect fasting and prayer and serve more time before their television images than before Your throne. They neglect the poor and live in splendor caring more about what others think of them than what You think. They neglect even the simplest works of charity, spending their substance on clothing, jewelry, motorized vehicles, and palatial houses. They corrupt themselves with constant exposure to violence, adultery, greed, fornication, and drunkenness. If You are counting on them to save Your precious world, I would do what you did in the time of Noah and remove them, find a godly seed, if You can, and make a new beginning."

"You'd love that, wouldn't you? You have not seen My patience. You work so hard to corrupt all that I have made. Should I not give those who have sworn allegiance to My name the opportunity to turn from their wicked ways? You know not what tomorrow brings forth. Throughout the globe there are hospitals, feeding centers, orphanages, and dedicated men and women serving at their own expense to bring My love forth into the planet, trying to repair what you constantly reap: death, destruction, broken homes, broken lives. My followers are not perfect, but they are becoming so, and when they become so, that is when you fear them most because they fear not their own death. You asked Me to withdraw the guardians from Brian Phillips, but he has not fallen. He continues to follow me."

"Anyone would. He lives in luxury, drives the latest model vehicle, is married to a beautiful woman, and is inventive and intelligent. Take something away from him and see if he still serves You. He will curse You and die. He serves You only for what You have done for him, not for who You are, Mighty One. He is just as weak as all the others are. Take his wife and see if he still serves You."

"Santero, you see only the outward. I alone see into the heart. I know that those who serve Me do so out of love. Now depart from My presence. It still saddens Me to see how grotesque you have become, serving your own fallen nature. His wife has a free will. She will stay or leave of her own decision. Your darkness casts an evil shadow over the beauty of all I have made."

CHAPTER TEN

TRANSFER OF SPIRITS

Humans remain ignorant of the simplest of the Mighty One's governing laws and principles, ignorantly thinking that they exist not to make life better, but to limit personal freedoms and choice. Nowhere is that thinking so prevalent as in the matter of extramarital sexual relationships, and Mia didn't have the faintest idea what was right or what was wrong.

She was beyond beautiful, and as Wedge Harwood had a living fantasy about oriental women, the chance to bring their relationship into the carnal realm was his dream.

Wedge flew over on the United Airlines midnight flight from Hong Kong, which actually put him in San Francisco at noon the next day. He thought it was strange that Mia had insisted he come alone and told him she was to be picking him up.

He couldn't miss her standing there, waiting for him. Every male eye in the terminal was directed toward her waist-length black hair and perfectly proportioned figure wearing a Donna Karen skirt split to the top of her thighs, revealing flawless white skin. Her face was absolute perfection, with a defined nose in perfect symmetry and eyes of deep green. In front, her hair draped her abundant bosoms upon which rode a breathtaking strand of natural pearls, each one nearly priceless. She acted as if the attention she garnered meant nothing to her and reached out to help Wedge with one of his small carry-ons, kissing his cheek.

"Hi, Wedge," she spoke.

"How's the project coming?" he asked nonchalantly about the Imps.

"Right on schedule."

He reacted to her holding his arm with a little surprise, but decided to play along to see where everything was headed.

"I didn't have time to book you a room, but I've got several extra at my place. You don't mind, do you? Are you tired?"

"No, I slept like a baby on the plane," Wedge spoke. "I didn't eat, though. Can we get something?"

"Sure, there's a great seafood place on the way."

Wedge couldn't pinpoint what was different about Mia. He hadn't seen her for about six weeks, but something had radically changed. It was as if he was being lured into some trap, but it was something he wanted more than life itself—the chance to be with Mia. Power beauty all wrapped into one package. He knew he'd give anything to be with her, and yet she was the one doing the chasing.

All through lunch, she flirted with him telling him how great he looked and how glad she was to have him supervising the new factory. She made him feel important and indispensable, as if without him Tannersly would be a contract labor sweat shop. They had several Polynesian style drinks and she was a little giddy behind the wheel of her Mercedes sky blue 560 which still managed to pull deftly into the garage of her huge concrete and steel palace overlooking the wind-swept beach. Her property was bordering a small state seal preserve and was virtually in isolation from the ever-expanding metropolis.

Mia couldn't explain to herself how different she felt. She had grown used to another presence living within her. She called it her second self, constantly giving her advice and insight into the different people she had to deal with. She knew there were people she could manipulate subversively and others that she couldn't. She knew that people were intrigued by her oriental beauty, but her magnetism was far beyond the sexual power a beautiful woman commanded. Every cell in her bristled with energy. She poured a few Mai

Tais from her wet bar and walked out onto the deck overlooking the Pacific.

"I made them just like my mother showed me," she smiled seductively.

Wedge was powerless to resist her advances and he was reluctant to as well. He felt her warm lips on his neck and her silk blouse push up against him. He turned his head and bent down to kiss her with full passion.

It was electrifying. A rush of energy seemed to engulf him, and he dropped with her to deck when they began to grapple with their clothing. He felt himself sinking into a warm vat of honey as they consummated their union.

"Wedge, Wedge," Mia cried, "it feels so good. Don't stop—don't."

Her hand dug into his back, leaving bruises, but he was oblivious. He began to choke as if he was being swallowed alive. Santero's spirit moved freely throughout Wedge's cornering his own spirit back into the recesses of his subconscious mind.

It was a pain that Wedge had never experienced. Every nerve ending throbbed and he found himself thinking he was all-powerful, invincible, and could conquer anything. He looked at Mia lying undressed and he felt contempt for her trying to use him as her pawn. He savagely racked her back and bit her about the chest and neck. She cried with pain and he ignored her. He was only concerned with his own sense of power and cared nothing for her suffering. He rose abruptly from the deck and looked at her.

"I'm going inside," he spoke, wondering why the sound of his own voice was so strange to him.

Wedge was to waste no time in getting the project going. When Mia came in the room, she found him on the phone. "We need to speed up the completion of the factory. I don't care where you get the workers from, just get them." He glanced up at Mia and put down the phone. "We're going to need those microprocessors almost immediately. Are they done?"

"Yes." Mia looked at him with wonderment, puzzled that she had stepped out of a position of control to subservience. "They're finished. It's just that we're modifying them for other languages and customs. We have a staff of linguists that are developing the European and Asian programming."

"So the ones that are in English are ready now," Wedge directed harshly. He grew impatient. "Well, damn it, I need to know whether they're ready or not."

"Yes," Mia reacted in shock. "What has come over you? You've never been like this before."

"I feel different," Wedge said as he stroked his chin. "It's nothing. I'm just damn sick of these delays and want to get these things into production. Look, I want to leave next week with at least a hundred thousand of the microprocessors. That won't be a problem, will it?"

"No," Mia said meekly, "it shouldn't be."

"Good," Wedge replied, "I need some rest. Will you show me to my room?"

* * * * *

Bruce Wainright was always happy to see his converts doing well and was even happier when they branched out on their own to do work for the Mighty One. Mario Rodriguez's recovery from gunshot wounds was a miracle the entire Bay Area talked about, and the satellite Alliance Christian Center he had established in Palo Alto was successful beyond any of his dreams. Mario had a vision for a gathering place where people of all races and social status could mingle together and worship the Mighty One. Open just a few short months, the building was already bursting beyond capacity and Bruce came down to visit and see what help the main congregation in San Mateo—also struggling from overcrowding—could offer.

"Brother Bruce," Mario greeted him enthusiastically, "I see you found me. We started this day care for the mothers in the church who wanted to finish their education and give their children a better shot. You like it?"

The room was sparsely furnished. Fifteen toddlers and infants were crawling on the tattered carpet. Most of the toys were missing parts and looked like Goodwill castaways. Three older grandmother types were reading stories and tending to the children.

"It's great," Bruce smiled. "Show me the rest of your place."

Mario gave him the grand tour which lasted about five minutes. He showed Bruce the sanctuary, basketball court, and brought him back into his small apartment adjacent to the sanctuary.

"How many services are you running now?" Bruce inquired.

"We've got a Saturday night and three Sundays. I don't think I could do another one. We're turning people away. Sometimes we open the windows and crowds just gather outside. You want to go with me?" Mario pulled out a packet of cards. "I'm going to visit some people who dropped in on us last weekend."

"Sure," Bruce said, "let's go out for lunch too."

Mario's 57 Chevy pulled up in front of the condo owned by Brian and Alice Phillips. He looked at the car. "Boy, these two married young. She's only 17 and he's 16. Looks like they're doing all right for themselves." They knocked on the door.

Alice was surprised to see two men standing outside her door but opened it up to them. "Hi, what can I do for you?"

"I'm Pastor Mario Rodriguez. You visited our church last weekend, so I'm returning the favor. Can we come in?

This is Bruce Wainright, senior minister. I was saved in his church and he's down helping me scout for a new building."

"Sure, I'm just fixing something for lunch—chicken salad. Would you like some?" Alice inquired. "It really won't be any trouble. I've only been married a short while and I think my husband is getting tired of being a guinea pig for my cooking recipes."

"Yeah," Bruce said, "it sounds great. This is a beautiful place you have. Is your husband home?"

Alice called out from the kitchen, "No, he's working on a new computer for Tannersly Industries. Between school and his job, he's barely home at all." Alice returned carrying a tray of iced tea. "Here, have some iced tea while I get the chicken salad served. You don't mind eating on our porch, do you? It's so different from Maine, so sunny. It's no wonder so many people live in California."

"Isn't Tannersly the company that made the furballs? Why are they switching to computer products?" Mario asked.

"I guess they feel there's a lot of money to be made." Alice was interrupted by the phone ringing.

"Oh hi, Brian. Some people are over visiting from the church."

"I left my folder on the bureau. Could you take a cab and bring it over?" Brian asked.

"Right now? I'm just making lunch. How about in an hour? Will that be all right?" Alice smiled. "Okay, I'll see you then."

"That was my husband. He left an important folder here. He's really brilliant. He doesn't like to show off, but it's a wife's privilege. Let me show you something." Alice set the chicken salad in front of them and went to the closet and pulled out a metal trunk no bigger than a makeup kit. Mario and Bruce watched wide-eyed as she pulled Louie out of the box and sat him on the table.

"Hi Louie," Alice said. "How are you doing today?"

"I'm fine," Louie responded. "Who are you two?" he asked, directing his attention to Mario and Bruce.

"I'm Mario Rodriguez, dude," Mario quipped. "You're the first lobster I've ever heard speak."

"Well, you're the first Mario I've ever spoken to." Louie turned his head in the direction of the chicken salad. "Alice, you're not serving lobster salad again, are you? Think of my poor cousins."

Bruce chuckled, "No, she's not."

"I know she's not. She's serving chicken salad prepared with mayonnaise and a bit of vinegar, celery salt over iceberg lettuce," Louie spoke proudly. "I can identify over 500 different smells. Who are you?"

"Reverend Bruce Wainright." Bruce put forward his hand. "I'd shake hands with you but I'd like to keep all of my fingers."

"Louie, we're going to eat," Alice spoke. "Now I'm going to put you back in your box."

"Please mom," Louie mimicked as Alice picked him up, "don't put me back in the box. No, anywhere, but not back in the box."

Alice put Louie back in the box and into the closet. She looked at Mario and Bruce who were quite speechless.

"What do you think?" Alice spoke proudly. "My husband made him when he was only 11. He's been taught thousands of responses and speaks seven languages. He'll even remember who are the next time he meets you. He's already programmed your face, voice pattern, and smell."

"Wow," Mario uttered, "your husband must be a genius. This chicken salad is good too."

"He's here on full scholarship. He's supposed to be working for Tannersly part-time, but they've got him more than I do. You might say he's married to his job and I'm his mistress, though trying not to be a jealous one."

"Are you planning on coming back to the church, Mrs. Phillips?" Bruce asked.

"Yes, we both thought it was great. Brian has been a Christian for a little over two years, and myself, well, since about age eight. My dad passed away this year, so rather than wait till Brian finished college, we decided to get married young. I guess we could both use some friends. Excuse me, I have to call a cab. Brian wants me to run some of his paperwork down to him and I haven't gotten another car yet."

"Why don't you let us drive you?" Mario spoke. "We're just out looking for new building sites. We won't mind at all taking you there and back."

"Okay, it would be nice for Brian to meet you as well. He's still not the best at working with strangers. He was quite an oddity when he was younger." Alice stood up. "I'm going to get ready. You two help yourselves to more."

CHAPTER ELEVEN

THE CONFRONTATION

Rahil resembled a large, overgrown werewolf. His eyes were a fiery liquid red and his fur was a bluish-cast black that looked blacker than midnight in a forest. He had been summoned by Santero after Santero had entered Mia Tannersly and then Wedge Harwood. The morning after engaging in sex with Wedge, Mia had felt free for the first time. The voices, the anger, the hatred, and feelings of filthiness were gone. She reflected for the first time remorsefully how she had destroyed the life of Chun Lee and wished she could somehow make up for it. Unknown to her, While Wedge was passed out on her king-sized Somabed, Santero had traveled to Egypt and had unbound Rahil and Nefroties to bring them back to possess Mia, from whom Marmorphis had departed.

Mia was startled when she looked into her bathroom mirror while brushing her luxurious hair. She was greeted by stares from Rahil's eyes, which beckoned her to enter the mirror. She was nearly hypnotized by Rahil's eyes but was distracted when she saw Nefroties appear alongside him. She was beautiful and had the most distinctive face Mia had ever seen.

"Come," Rahil beckoned, extending his huge paw almost through the mirror, "join us."

Mia was entranced. She looked closer into the mirror and saw beyond them a seemingly endless cavern.

"We offer the secret of life, eternal life and beauty," Nefroties spoke.

"Who are you?" Mia spoke to the mirror. "What do you want with me?"

"You re beautiful," Nefroties said, "but already you are beginning to wrinkle. Look into my face. I am thousands of years old."

Mia looked closer and closer until she could see her very breath ebbing on the mirror. She stepped back in horror as Rahil opened his mouth and revealed his fangs.

"Ha ha ha ha ha," Rahil laughed. He vaporized out of the mirror and ascended like smoke up her nostrils, where she found herself gasping for air. She pushed herself away from the sink and struggled for life, finding hers ebbing away. Nefroties glared out of the mirror.

"Yes, you shall have eternal beauty, but only because it will be me dwelling in your body."

Nefroties swirled about and burrowed into Mia's abdomen, filling her lower body region.

Mia was lost in a deep, dark dream as Rahil glared out of her eyes at the world around him. The body returned to the sleeping form of Wedge Harwood and shook it awake.

Santero glared back out of Wedge Harwood's eyes.

"It is completed," Mia spoke in a lower range.

"Nefroties as well?" Wedge questioned, grabbing Mia's hand and pulling her to the bed.

Another voice arose out of Mia. "Yes, I am here as well. What is it you wish, Lord Santero?"

"Show me how it was you seduced your Ramses with your beauty."

Wedge pulled Mia to the bed and climbed on top of her. He was thrown back into the headboard.

"Not you, Rahil. Let the spirit of Nefroties manifest."

It was a good thing that Mia's house was perched on a bluff overlooking the ocean and that her nearest neighbor was more than 300 yards away. Otherwise, they surely would have reported to the police what had happened that morning. As Mia dug her nails into Wedge's back and sliced it with her razor-sharp fingernails, he let out screams that would have sent chills down the spine of even the toughest KGB interrogator. Their mating was like a union of two rabid wolves, thrashing, clawing, biting, and throwing one another around the room until the sheets were matted with bits of hair, blood, and skin. The host physical bodies collapsed in exhaustion, the energies having been fully depleted.

That day at Tannersly Industries, no one could help but notice Mia's physical condition. The left side of her face was bruised and her lips were swollen. She had worn an ankle-length skirt and a long-sleeved, high-collar blouse. Otherwise they would have seen the multiple bruises and scratch marks.

"Good morning, Ms. Tannersly," April Adams, the receptionist, greeted her. "Did you have a good weekend?"

"Yes," Mia replied in a low voice, which startled April, "very rewarding. Is Brian Phillips here?"

"Yes, he's in with our engineering department." She looked at her strangely. "Is something wrong with your voice?"

"No, nothing's wrong with my voice," Mia snapped. "Is something wrong with your hearing? Tell Mr. Phillips the minute he's done, I need to see him. Get an identification badge for Mr. Harwood from Hong Kong. He came in last night and is to be given full facility clearance." She pulled out a passport. "He doesn't like to have his picture taken, so just have them make a copy of his passport photo."

"What about voice identification?" she inquired. "Will he be able to furnish us with a tape?"

"No, just call him at my home number and tape it. Then give it to Walter."

Rahil didn't have the faintest inkling about computers or anything else about modern technology, but he knew Santero was crazy about them and was planning on using much of them to rule the world. He knew periodically he'd have to descend into her subconscious and allow her to consciously operate Tannersly, which was of tantamount importance to Santero. He didn't like it— especially occupying the same body as Nefroties.

He loathed Nefroties. She had been responsible for getting him bound in the first place. She had influenced Ramses not to let the Hebrew children go back to their homeland. Rahil hadn't cared either way. He knew the power of the Hebrew God and would have been happier with the children of Jacob gone. He had battled with Nefroties for control of the Pharaoh's heart, but she had won, having influenced him through his queen. After the death of the Pharaoh's son, the Pharaoh had cursed him and he remained in bonds for thousands of years until Santero had set him free to possess Mia. Rahil hated Nefroties and would get even with her when given even the slightest opportunity.

Brian came out of his meeting and found a message from Andrea, his secretary, to see Mia immediately. He walked into his office to pick up his laptop to show Mia what progress had been made. He was feeling bad because of the recent way he had been getting along with Alice and made a special mental note to compliment her when she came to bring him the folder he left at home.

Yoballa was the guardian assigned to Bruce and many other members of the Alliance Christian Church. Even while Bruce, Mario, and Alice were driving over, he could feel the confrontation coming. Mario bowed his head to pray silently in the back seat and Raphael appeared on the scene with Uzziah.

"You know Santero is back," Yoballa spoke, showing no fear in his voice.

"Yes," Raphael interjected, "I can sense his presence. I don't know fully why because the Mighty One has not revealed all, but I know he wants to destroy Brian Phillips. He personally requested that Uzziah and I be withdrawn as his guardians."

"The Mighty One alone knows the beginning from the end," Ballelulia said. "I trust that he has laid another trap that will thwart Santero's plans for destruction. We are fortunate that we are amongst humans that know the power of prayer. I feel like I could move a mountain."

Raphael smiled, "I know the feeling. I have had to move a few myself. Perhaps it will be better if Yoballa confronts him by himself. We could come to his aid if so need be."

Uzziah flew alongside. "That it up ahead—Tannersly. We will wait out here. If you need assistance, Yoballa, sing. We will join you."

Mario parked in the front of the building in the guest parking section and they walked into the lobby. They were greeted by the receptionist, who looked them over suspiciously.

"May I be of help?" she queried.

"I'm Alice Phillips. These are two friends of mine. I'm here to drop off something for my husband. These two were kind enough to drive me down here . . ."

The receptionist interrupted Alice. "Just a minute." They stood waiting while she was on the phone, looking around at the marble foyer and the strange Chinese art work.

"Looks demonic," Mario said.

"This place always gives me the creeps," Alice said. "Something about it just doesn't feel right."

"You may go in. He's in the conference room at the end of the hall."

The hall was much darker than anyone would have intended. Before they got to the large double oak door, Bruce grabbed his side in pain and doubled over.

"Ohhh," he said, resting against the wall.

"Are you all right?" Alice asked, leaning over him. "It's so hot in here."

"Yoballa, so we haven't seen the last of you," Santero challenged. "You may have defeated my plans last time, but this time nothing will stop me. I don't suppose you've met Rahil."

Yoballa looked at Rahil, who towered over him, and was unable to ward off the blow to his midsection.

"You servant of the Weak One, don't you know this planet and its inhabitants are ours? You lack the power to remove us from our high places. We serve at their invitation," he laughed, trying to slash him again.

Yoballa took his light rope and threw it about Rahil's paw that was coming to slash him in the face.

"Our weapons are not carnal, as yours are. Our weapons are eternal."

Rahil struggled with the light rope which singed his fur, binding his claws together. Rahil lunged towards Yoballa howling in pain with his jaw open to bite Yoballa's head. Yoballa stood his ground and at the last minute, feigned left and ducked right, sending Rahil into his outstretched sword, which impaled his eye and caused Rahil to gasp in pain again.

"What of you, Santero?" Yoballa asked.

"You may pass, Yoballa. You are a worthy adversary. It's too bad that you chose to remain with the Mighty One. You could have accomplished much at my side. Even now, we will rule these earthlings as never before."

"I seek not the vain glory you seek, Santero. I seek the love of the Mighty One which runs through my very being."

"Bruce," Mario said, "are you okay?"

"Yeah," Bruce said, "there's some heavy spiritual warfare going on here. I don't know what it's about, but please don't quit praying."

"This is it," Alice said, opening the door. She looked in and saw Brian next to Wedge Harwood and Mia, who looked at her with a fierce seduction. She glanced back to her husband and put an obvious hand on his shoulder. Brian looked up at the visitors.

"Hi, Alice." He looked worried. "Who are your friends?"

Mario walked up, ignoring Mia and Wedge. "I'm Mario. We visited your home earlier and returned the favor for you coming to our church. This is our senior pastor, Bruce Wainright."

"Brian," Bruce said, extending his hand, "what type of work is it you do here? We met your friend, Louie. You are quite creative."

"It's not something he's allowed to discuss," Mia said, staring at him. "What church is it you're with?"

"Alliance Christian Center in San Mateo." Bruce pulled out a business card. "You're welcome to visit us anytime."

"I think not," Mia replied with a fiery look coming over her eyes. "Religion is for old people, people too weak to live their own lives. I'm not the superstitious kind. Live and let live."

"Well, sister," Mario interjected, looking at the opulent conference room, "you can surround yourself with luxuries but you can't find peace without God."

"I seem to have done all right." Wedge Harwood stood up wearing dark sunglasses and a sleek, steel blue silk suit with black alligator shoes. "I've got all the peace I need, preacher boy. Now I know you're a guest of Mrs. Phillips, but I think our philosophies are vastly different. Jesus to me was some weakling who allowed himself to be crucified when he could have ruled the world and had lots of people follow him. He could have lived in a palace. Now if you really ask me, I think he was a fool."

Brian walked over. "There's no need to start a religious war here. My wife has just come to give me my folder that I left at home. Alice, why don't you take our guests out?" He looked around and saw Wedge growing hotter and hotter.

Santero drew his nostrils back and spewed forth a black, pungent, sulfuric smoke. "Curses on you, Yoballa, guardian of the meek, protector of the weak." A fire bolt hit Yoballa in the arm; he grimaced in pain. "See how the Mighty One will cure you from my wrath."

Yoballa took his light band and lassoed Santero; the bands melted around his waist.

"You have no power over me, Yoballa," Santero said, approaching him to deal a mortal blow.

Yoballa lifted his voice in song, "Praise to the Mighty One, praise to the omnipotent Creator."

Raphael and Ballelulia materialized by his side. Raphael stepped up and sliced at Santero, catching him on the jaw. "We should even the odds a bit, Santero."

"Raphael, up to your tricks, hiding in the bushes until your appearance is needed."

"I like to know who I'm up against," Raphael retorted, swinging his sword and backsiding Santero with the blade, all the while keeping an eye on Rahil and Nefroties.

"You have no right here. No one has invited you. This land and these people are ours."

"You have spoken wrongly, Nefroties. Not only do you look foolish garbed as a woman, but indeed, you speak foolishly." Ballelulia wrapped Nefroties in a light band so that he was immobilized. "The earth is the Lord's and all herein. You are the trespassers."

* * * * *

"You are absolutely right, Brian. Wedge, please don't harass our engineer's friends. He wishes to go to church, and it is his prerogative to believe in Jesus Christ. I'm sorry, Reverend, that your reception here has been less than cordial. Perhaps I will accept your invitation after all to visit your church. Now perhaps you'll excuse us so we can continue our meeting. And please excuse Mr. Harwood as well. He has recently arrived from China and perhaps is not experienced in our Western courtesies."

Mia extended her hand to shake hands with Mario and Bruce. She smiled sweetly at Alice.

"No harm done, Miss Tannersly," Bruce said. "Good luck with your new project. Come on, Alice, we'll give you a ride back to your house."

"I'll be home early, Alice," Brian offered, wondering how the whole episode had started, to begin with.

Brian arrived home dead tired. The session with Mia and Wedge had drained him of all energy. The design he had come up with for the new microprocessor was too expensive, so he was ordered to redesign it using fewer chips. He opened the door and called out for Alice. She wasn't anywhere around. He wandered into the kitchen and found a note from her explaining that she was at a church newcomers' dinner. There was a ready-to-eat meal left for him in the refrigerator. The phone rang just as he reached for the refrigerator door.

"Brian, hi. You dad and I are coming out next weekend," his mom said. "What are you doing?"

"I was just getting ready to heat up some dinner," Brian said, reaching in the refrigerator and pulling out the dish.

"How are your classes going?" Brenda asked. "Any new developments from my genius son?"

"Yeah, I finished the prototype for Tannersly and they scrapped it—said it would be too expensive. I'm going to take one of my designs into my professor, Tom O'Brien. He used to work with Intel. Maybe he'll give me some insight."

"Where's Alice?" his mom asked, looking concerned.

"She's out at church. I can't blame her. I'm not giving her much of a life being gone to school and work all day," Brian complained. "I'm surprised she's stuck around this long."

"Well, don't get yourself down in the dumps," his mom advised. "Remember, life is not all work. It took a while after we were married to get your father to leave his all-important work and come with me to the Vineyard. Remember, life went on before you were here and it'll go on after you're gone. I'll let you get to your dinner."

As Brian sat eating his dinner alone, he reflected on his marriage to Alice, his classes, and Tannersly Industries. He realized that life was going to be what he made it! He'd already begun to feel owned by Tannersly. They were demanding more from him than what they were entitled to.

He wished for the comfort of Alice's companionship and knew that if he had to do it over again, the scene at the conference room would have turned out much differently. It dawned on him that what he was feeling from Wedge and Mia was a black coldness and a sinister evil, and he knew with all the knowledge within him that the very toy he was designing could be used for mass mind control of the most insidious nature. He went into the room and took out Louie. He plugged him into his MacIntosh and studied the microprocessor board. After pouring over it nearly two hours, he knew how to not only redesign the microprocessor to be more economical, but also how to prevent it from being used for evil purposes.

Alice came home from church breathless and beaming with energy. Mario escorted her to the door.

"Brian," Alice sang out, "I'm back."

Brian left the computer workstation and came into the living room where he saw Mario.

"Hi," Brian said, extending his hand, "thanks for giving my wife a ride home. Can I get you anything?"

No," Mario said, "we ate a lot—frijoles, ribs, chicken, coleslaw, tamales, tacos, chocolate cream pie. If I eat anything more, I think I'll burst like a piñata."

"Hey, I'm sorry about how you and the Reverend were treated today. It was really uncalled for." Brian sat down. "Have you been a Christian long?"

"Yeah, about a year and a half. I used to run with my own gang till Bruce let me know where it was at with the Mighty One. I've been trying to live 24 7 ever since."

"What do you mean twenty-four seven?"

"I live for Jesus 24 hours a day, 7 days a week. It's a habit, a good habit. Those people that you work for, they gave me the willies. The chick looked like an oriental Elvira and the dude like he was from the 'Night of the Living Dead.'"

Alice walked out of the bathroom and walked up to Brian, giving him a kiss. "I would have called you to let you know where I was, but I knew you were at school. Did you eat?" she asked, hopeful that he liked what she made for him.

"Yeah, did you make it yourself? It was great." He watched her eyes light up, just knowing that he had said what she wanted him to say. "You keep cooking like that and we're going to have to open our own high-class restaurant."

"Hey, look, you two haven't seen each other all day. Three's a crowd. We want to see you at church, brother," Mario said, slapping him a high five. "Gotta go."

With a little help from Professor O'Brien, Brian was able to rework the microprocessor to use fewer chips and still do as much. The manufacturing costs could be brought down significantly to less than $2.00 per unit because of the large volume Tannersly was ordering.

Without anyone's knowledge, Brian programmed a computer virus that would destroy the computer's functioning capacity. He fixed it so at 15 hertz for three seconds and 25 hertz for fifteen seconds all memory would be erased. The program was buried in the audio sensor chip with a hidden relay stored in the capacitor. He wasn't taking any chances on his toy being used for evil purposes.

He was excited that his parents were coming in and were planning on staying with them for several days. They had a whole itinerary worked out for the Bay Area, including a short trip to Alcatraz. Brian had always been fascinated with the "Bird Man." His classes gave him no trouble, and even though his professors had many years in their respected fields, he quickly mastered and tested out of nearly every class. He was looking forward to the debating season and the friends he would make in the debate class.

In his office alone, he instinctively reached for the phone to call Alice. "Hi, what are you doing?"

"I'm making dinner for your folks: crab alfredo, broccoli with hollandaise sauce and a Caesar salad. I'm in a dilemma on what kind of beverage to serve."

"Iced tea would be great," Brian quipped. "We wouldn't want you going back on the bottle and panhandling at Ghiradelli Square."

"Very funny. Speaking of panhandling, my stockbroker called. He said your company is trading very actively."

"Yeah, the word's out on the new toy. It's all favorable. They're testing it with some kids in Phoenix. In fact, next week they want me to go down and watch part of the tests."

"What about me?"

"You're invited too. We're a package deal. Where I go, you go. I'll be home after I pick up my folks."

The Stealth was hardly big enough for both of his parents, but they didn't complain about the crowded conditions and managed to talk his ear off all the way down to the house. He couldn't wait to show his parents the prototype Imp just shipped to him from China.

The production facility in China was working at full tempo day and night. After the mold stamped out the plastic parts for the Imps, the conveyor belts took them to the platform of workers that put in the metal skeleton that gave them their movement. Then they were transported to a high-tech building where they were fitted with their microprocessors. Wedge had flown back making sure that each of the Imps was inhabited by small ones. They were happy to be out of their darkness and they wasted no time in learning how to manipulate the on-board computer processor.

Lubato, the leader of the small ones, was in awe at the presence of Santero. Eons ago he had changed from a worshipping cherub and rebelled against the Mighty One to follow Santero. Having spent so much time in the outer darkness, he had many times regretted his decision, but he was still convinced that things would work out for all of them at the end. He knew that Santero was genius and that genius was wrapped up oftentimes in madness.

Santero's plan was a bold one: to throw the families of the world in confusion by pitting child against parents and brothers against sisters. The small ones were taught how to manipulate the voice chip to continually program their owners while the owners lay sleeping.

The test marketing in Phoenix had surpassed even Santero's wildest expectations. They had chosen 30 students from Carl Hayden Junior High School, located in a lower-income part of town. Each of the students had been given their own toy and were told to take it everywhere with them. The Imps were a sensation. Reporters had caught wind of it in spite of the strict security; they released the story over the national AP wire and triggered a sharp climb in the trading value of Tannersly Industries.

Darius Mendez was 12 and lived with his mom, Quanita, and baby sister Chelsea in a government-sponsored apartment that his mom paid only five dollars a month for. He loved toys and was fascinated by his Imp.

"Mom, look what the school gave me." He couldn't wait to show her the Imp the day he received it.

"You lyin' to me, son? You been stealin' again?" she challenged him while she changed his baby sister's diapers. "If you are, you're gonna be sorry."

"No, I swear it. Call the school. A company wants us to test them. They call it marketing." He pulled a paper out of his school bag. "Here's the paper I'm supposed to fill out."

He showed her the paper in English, which she could barely read, but she made a pretense of it anyway and shoved it back at him. "Well, all right, you can keep it, but keep it out of the way."

"It's not an 'it.' I named him Oogie. Tell my mom hi, Oogie."

"Hi mom," Oogie said. "What's that smell? Smells like poop!"

She gave a shocked look. "It is. How'd you know that? You're just a toy."

"No, I'm not. I'm Oogie. I'm your new son. Go ahead, ask me anything."

"Okay, Oogie, I suppose you can tell fortunes too," Mrs. Mendez said, challenging him.

"What fortune would you like me to tell?" Oogie asked.

"Oogie, can you really tell fortunes?" Darius asked incredulously. "Really?"

"Oogie can do many things. I can smell, hear, talk. You have someone coming to your door right now—someone with big feet."

Everyone paused and there was a knock on the door. Chelsea started crying and Darius answered it.

"Hi, Mr. Martin," Darius said. "Mom, it's Mr. Martin."

"Tell him to fix our sink. How am I supposed to cook for you kids with the plumbing backed up?"

"We've got to bring in a crew with jackhammers and dig up the whole sewer line. We were sort of hoping you could leave for like a day. Do you got a relative you could visit—like tomorrow?"

"Yeah, we'll leave," Mrs. Mendez said nastily. "Just get it fixed or I'll call the Department of Human Services and tell them just what a rat hole you're renting here."

"Thank you, Mrs. Mendez," Mr. Martin said. "Have a good day, Darius. What's that?"

"I'm Oogie. Mr. Martin, just fix the sink."

Darius closed the door before Mr. Martin could say anything else.

That night while Darius slept, Oogie's controls were turned on by Lubato, who began to chant, "Kill your little sister, kill your little sister, kill your little sister, kill your little sister."

Darius dreamt of taking his sister and holding her underwater. He found himself smiling as she gulped for her last breath, giving up and sinking into unconsciousness and death. He awoke.

"Good morning, Darius," Oogie said. "Are you going to school today? I think your mom is making food. Are you going to take me with you?"

"Yeah, Oogie, I thought you weren't supposed to talk unless you're talked to," Darius said.

"Have I offended you, Darius?" Oogie apologized.

"No," Darius said, "I wish my little sister would quit crying all the time. It really is beginning to get under my nerves."

Lubato was delighted. It had worked. Only one night and Darius was already irritated with his little sister. Santero's plan was brilliant.

That day Jimmy Fulton never made it to class. In the middle of the night, without any explanation, he went into his mother's room and stabbed her to death. When they carted him off to juvenile detention center, he could offer no explanation except that he was mad at her for not buying him a new bike. The police were baffled. No one made the connection that he was part of the select test group—no one, except Mia, who was staying in Phoenix to personally supervise the testing.

The next day Charlene Andrews scalded her baby brother with hot water, sending him to the emergency unit at St. Luke's Hospital, where he was listed in critical condition. She swore it must have been an accident, but the amount of water and severity of the burns made her story hard for anyone to believe.

That Friday, Darius's mom left him in charge of his baby sister while she went to the store to take advantage of a sale on tortillas. While she was gone, Chelsea began to cry.

"Shut up, Chelsea," Darius challenged, "unless you want something to really cry about."

Chelsea was wide eyed as Darius came over.

"Shut up, Chelsea," Oogie said. "You're just a little dirt bag. Shut up if you know what's good for you."

Oogie rolled over to where Darius was watching television. Chelsea continued to cry.

"Make her shut up, Darius," Oogie chanted. "Shut up, shut up, shut up."

The crying got worse. Darius got mad, picked up the television changer, and threw it at his sister. It hit her and made her really howl. He walked over to her with a big pillow and started to smother her. She began to cry in terror as she gasped for breath. Right before she went into unconsciousness, Mr. Martin showed up at the door.

"Anybody home?" He knocked and let himself in. "What are you doing to your sister, Darius?" He saw Darius sitting on top of his sister, choking off her breath. He grabbed Darius by the shoulders and threw him off. Chelsea was nearly unconscious. He took her into his arms and set her down on the couch.

She lay on the couch gasping, "Mamma, mamma, mamma."

"What are you, an animal?" Mr. Martin screamed. "Killing your own sister!"

Mrs. Mendez walked into the apartment carrying a package of groceries.

"Chelsea, Chelsea," she shouted, running over to her daughter. "What happened?"

"I came to the door and found your son trying to kill his sister."

"Mom, she was crying. I wasn't trying to kill her—just trying to keep her quiet. Honestly."

"Get yourself ready for school now. We're going to talk with the school counselor."

Mia opened her morning paper that was delivered with her coffee and croissant at the Arizona Biltmore. She noticed the news reports of Jimmy Fulton stabbing his mother and Charlene Andrews scalding her baby brother. She checked her list of test students from the school and smiled unconsciously. She reached for the phone and called Wedge. She reached him right before he was going to bed.

"Wedge, it's working. The children are already beginning to respond to our programming. How soon until you're ready to ship?"

"We're right on target and should be able to ship the first hundred thousand units into Long Beach Harbor this week. They're loading them today. No problems. Anyone making the connection?"

"No, nobody at all," Mia said, sipping her coffee. "Look, I think our test is over. I'm going back to Palo Alto. The Phillips boy is making some additional programming changes for me."

"He doesn't suspect anything, does he?" Wedge inquired.

"No, not at all. I felt it would be wise to leave him out of any direct contact with our test subjects," Mia responded, polishing her long nails with a file until they were razor sharp. "When are you coming in?"

"I'll be there when the shipment comes in. I personally want to make sure nothing goes wrong. Do you have the paperwork done for the first order?"

"Yes, all hundred thousand are going to stores in California. We have orders for 300,000 more and the toy show isn't until next month. This is going to be the biggest pre-Christmas toy ever. I'll see you when you get here."

Mia hung up the phone and began to pack. She pretty much just went through the motions of living her life. She was being suffocated by Rahil and Nefroties and could feel the constant turmoil of them grappling for control of her.

"When Santero comes back, we'll see who's in charge," Nefroties taunted. "You're nothing but a bag of fur, Rahil."

"Santero only wants you for one thing, Nefroties, and it's not your intelligence. I possessed her first. You may have your moments of influence, but it is I who commands her life. See how she sharpens her nails? As sharp as my teeth. Why don't you leave and find your own host? I grow tired of sharing this body with you. Have you nowhere else to go? These quarters grow more and more cramped."

Mia had to fight off the urge to scratch her face. She turned away from the mirror, knowing she was hopelessly trapped. She thought of the joy on the faces of Bruce and Mario and wondered if she could experience the same joy by attending their church. She knew that whatever was happening inside of her, something was amiss. It was a rare moment of lucidity, and as she looked into her pupils, she saw two pairs of eyes looking back, challenging . . .

CHAPTER TWELVE

OOGIE

Mrs. Mendez dragged Darius by the shirt sleeve into the office of Dr. Lloyd Ziegler, the school counselor. He was 38 and a member of a large church where he had first worked as a church counselor before receiving his state certificate, which allowed him to practice in the school systems. He rotated from school to school, helping dysfunctional children from dysfunctional homes. He had keen insight into problems and relied on the Mighty One for daily wisdom and guidance. He looked up to see Mrs. Mendez dragging in her son, who was holding Oogie.

"Have a seat." Dr. Ziegler said, rising. "I understand from my secretary that you have a problem with Darius."

Darius sat on the sofa across from him, holding Oogie on his lap.

"Who is that with you, Darius?" Dr. Ziegler asked.

"My name is Oogie," Oogie said. "It's nice to meet you, Dr. Ziegler. You're wearing my favorite cologne, Polo."

"How do you know that, Oogie?" Lloyd asked, wondering. "How do you even know my name?"

"It's printed on that notebook. I can see it from here. Graduate Thesis of Lloyd Ziegler. Dysfunctional Children, Product of Dysfunctional Homes."

"Very good." Dr. Ziegler ended his banter with Oogie and turned to Darius. "I understand that you tried to kill your sister earlier. Your mom told me over the phone that you adore your baby sister. Why now, Darius? What did she do that made you want to suffocate her?"

"I don't know," Darius began to blubber. "I was just trying to get her to keep quiet. I wasn't going to kill her."

"Well, maybe you weren't intending to kill her, but something inside you snapped, Darius." Dr. Ziegler put his hand on Darius's shoulder. "You can't sit on top of a little child with a pillow over her mouth and expect her to survive."

"I swear, Dr. Ziegler, I didn't want to kill anybody. I love Chelsea."

"How long have you had Oogie?" Dr. Ziegler asked.

"Just a little while." Darius looked up, wiping the tears from eyes. "I named him myself."

"I understand all of the children in your class were given these toys," Dr. Ziegler reflected. "Mrs. Mendez, I don't think your daughter is in any immediate danger, at least not right now. But under no circumstances should you leave her alone with your son. There has been a rash of child-related crimes just in the past several days. I don't want to add another victim to the list."

Ziegler reflected on the Imps. Perhaps, in some way, the toys could be connected with the recent outbreak of youthful violence. He shook off the notion as being too absurd and decided there must be some other cause for the random violence. What was happening in Phoenix was no different than what was happening in most of the country as thousands of preschoolers were exposed to a constant diet of violence and murder. They were simply imitating in real life what they had seen on television.

"Tell me, Oogie," Ziegler directed his question, "where were you when Darius was choking Chelsea?"

"I was not in the room. Darius left me in his room," Oogie said.

"Did you tell Darius to choke his sister?" Ziegler directed.

"No, I love Darius. I would not want him to do anything he does not want to do. I am Darius's friend, his friend always. I will help Darius."

"Very well. I know you are a computer, a robot, but tell me, how do you learn? Who has taught you?" Ziegler asked.

"I have been given memory chips with much knowledge. I can have my knowledge renewed by database from Tannersly Industries."

Ziegler decided to try and trick Oogie. "Who were you before you were Oogie?"

Lubato fell for the bait. He was proud of who he was and was getting tired of assuming the personality of the robot. Before he realized what he was doing, he responded, "I am Lubato, ruler of the small ones."

Darius looked over in shock. "You told me you were Oogie!"

"I am Oogie as well, but my real name is Lubato," he said.

"What does that mean?" Ziegler asked. "You rule over the small ones. Who are the small ones?"

"The small ones are those who serve Santero in religious statues throughout the Far East. We are many."

Ziegler wished he had his tape recorder on. He turned to Mrs. Mendez, "I don't think it is a good idea for you to let your son continue to play with Oogie. He may not be all he seems to be."

"Mom, I love Oogie. He's my best friend, my only friend. I don't want to give up Oogie," Darius pleaded.

"Doctor, do you have any proof at all that Oogie is bad for Darius? Or is it just your medical suspicions? We're not a rich family. I cannot go and buy many toys for Darius as other moms and dads can," Mrs. Mendez directed, rising from her seat. "I'll watch my son a little more closely, but I don't see how a toy, especially one as smart as Oogie, can be causing these problems. Now I'd like to excuse myself, if you don't mind."

Dr. Ziegler stood and shook hands with Mrs. Mendez. "Thank you for coming in. I'll be checking on Darius and I do hope you'll come back as well."

Ziegler watched them walk out of his office. He picked up the phone to call his old college buddy who had moved to

California to start a church. "Bruce," he said, "it's Lloyd. Say, do you have a few minutes? I've got a problem down here."

Ziegler was shocked to find out that Bruce was familiar with Tannersly Industries and that one of the newest members of the church had helped develop the Imps. Bruce told him he was coming back to visit some friends the next week and he would definitely get together with him.

The fallen began to manifest themselves more and more. Bobby Morris had named his toy "Doogie," after Doogie Hauser, his hero on television. Like Doogie, he wanted to be a doctor and had assembled his own instruments that he had procured from his mom's silverware drawer and his dad's workshop. Doogie kept a pretty low profile, and just recently, he suggested to Bobby that he dissect the family cat.

Melvin the cat had wandered in leerily to Bobby's backyard playhouse. Bobby had tied him to the operating table and had begun to cut into him when the neighbor girl, Lisa Morrell, 15 years old and an animal lover, came in. She let out a scream which had stopped Bobby cold.

"What are you doing to your cat, Bobby?" She reached over and grabbed the knife away from him. "You're a monster."

In the background, Doogie mimicked her, "You're a monster, Bobby." Doogie laughed.

"You shut up," Lisa said to Doogie. "You're some sick robot."

Lisa picked up Melvin and cradled him in her arms. The hair was already shaved off his hindquarters and he hissed at even being touched.

"I'm showing your parents what you did to this cat, Bobby. You're going to be sorry, I promise you. They should lock people up like you and throw away the key."

"Go ahead and tell them," Bobby challenged boldly. "See if I care."

Later that night, Lisa came over to the Morris's home after dinner. She rang the doorbell and Bobby answered.

"Where are your parents?" she demanded. "I need to see them."

"Where's Melvin?" Bobby said. "I told my parents you took him."

"That's a lie," Lisa protested, "and you know it."

"You'd better go," Bobby said, gloating. "If you don't get off my porch, I'm telling my parents I saw you messing around with Melvin. Everyone in this neighborhood knows you're a meddler."

Lisa stormed off the porch, totally frustrated. She decided to keep Melvin for herself and nurse him back into shape. She vowed to somehow get even with little Bobby Morris.

That Sunday, Alice and Brian went to the main Alliance Christian Church in San Mateo. They got there early and grabbed a seat by the front. The choir started slowly rocking back and forth, keeping time with their hands as the drummer and bass player kicked in adding punch to their phrasing. The congregations around Alice and Brian rose to their feet and began to shout, "Alleluia." A young fellow with a zig-zag cut into the side of his head mounted the platform and began to rap:

"If you think the Mighty One's too deaf to hear
Brother let me tell you that the time is near.
He'll answer your prayers yes or no
Or maybe even later that's the way it goes.
Don't expect Him to jump to your every whim
He's the creator, so confess your sins.
If you're sitting high and mighty, like you're someone cool,
Remember without His wisdom, you're just a fool."

Brian felt his heart being touched throughout the song service. When Bruce finally got up to speak, Brian reached over and touched Alice's hand. He whispered to her, "I've got to talk to him afterward."

Several times during the sermon, Bruce looked directly at them as he emphasized his points: the wisdom of the Mighty One versus the wisdom of men. The pride of accomplishment that Brian carried with him began to dissipate and he began to see how proud he was and how little he was in the sight of the Mighty One, who had formed the universe and regarded the world as dust in His hands. He thought of the artificial intelligence he had helped build for Tannersly Industries and the complexity of the world the Mighty One had formulated and how everything was laid out perfectly. He saw clearly for the first time the root of his rebellion, the refusal to accept money from Alice's trust funds and investments, refusal to allow his parents to give him wise counsel about getting married so young, and even his stupidity in going ahead and working on a project with so much potential to be misused by the wrong people—that could actually harm so many children.

Several people gathered around Bruce when he was done. Brian and Alice waited their turn, and Bruce greeted them warmly.

"Hi, Alice," Bruce hugged her. "I see you dragged your husband out of the laboratory."

"Can I have a word with you, Pastor?" Brian asked. "Something is on my mind."

"I'm leaving for Phoenix tomorrow," Bruce pointed out. "Why don't we talk right now? Would you like Alice to join us or is this a men only talk?"

"No," Brian reacted in surprise, "it's not a men only talk. It's about my job and what I've done."

They all sat down in Bruce's office, whose walls were lined with Bible commentaries and a map of the Holy Land, along with several other photos of the California coastline.

"What's on your mind?" Bruce inquired.

"I'm not so sure that the toy I designed is going to be good for children. I mean, I helped with the microprocessor. I found the 164 megabyte chip, the BiCMOS, which has a faster speed and consumes less energy to promote longer battery life. So in a practical sense, I helped make this thing totally affordable."

"I don't understand much about computers, but that sounds like you put them on the right track. What seems to be the problem—the people you work with? Their attitudes?" Bruce said, looking right through him.

"Not just their attitudes, but what they plan on using the robots for. It comes off like they want to use them to entertain children, but I'm not even allowed to see the final product. They sent the processor boards to Korea where Samsung puts in the final chip. I don't know what they've programmed these things to do, so I planted a virus, just in case."

"Brian, you did what?" Alice asked, shocked. "You gave these things a virus? They're computers. How do computers get viruses?"

"It's not a bacteria. It's a signal that a programmer can give to wipe out all on-board memory."

"You know they are testing your toys in Phoenix, don't you?" Bruce asked.

"I heard they were, but they have me busy working on some programming applications. Besides, I can't get away from school." Brian looked at Bruce strangely. "How did you know we were doing a product test in Phoenix?"

"My old college friend, Lloyd Ziegler, had a run in with a lady whose son tried to choke his sister. Lloyd told me the kid was in the Tannersly Test Group and there were problems already with three of them from the test group trying to hurt family members. I told him I'd drop by when I was in Phoenix," Bruce added. "I'm leaving first thing in the morning."

"You going to meet the kid?" Alice asked.

"Yeah, but it's not just one child. They've given these to a test group of 30, all from the same grade school, and the problem seems to be spreading."

"Great. My first professional design job and it turns out like this." Brian looked down at the floor. "How did this ever happen?"

"Brian, the battles in this world are not against the seen, but the unseen." Bruce reached over and grabbed their hands. "I think it's time we enlist the help of the Mighty One on this and start a continual prayer chain."

CHAPTER THIRTEEN
BY THE TIME I GET TO . . .

Phoenix never looked better to Bruce as he flew over South Mountain, bursting with the colorful desert foliage, prickly pear and saguaro flowers, and verdant desert grasses. It was a virtual oasis to his eyes. He looked up at the "Seat Belt Fasten" sign and closed his eyes to ask for the Mighty One's help. Unknown to him, he was heading for a showdown with Wedge Harwood, who flew in the night before and was staying with Mia to further supervise the Imp project.

"You've got to get these things under control, Mia," Wedge directed. "You should never have put the entire test group in the same class." He threw down the morning paper with the headline: MOTHER AND CHILD KILLED BY TEN-YEAR-OLD.

The night before, Joey Bonita had been awaken by his Imp, who he had nicknamed Star. Star was chanting to him to kill his family. Star had been possessed by Wol, a fallen spirit who had lived in countless Buddhas and was able to extract total obedience. As Joey was sleeping, Wol vaporized into Joey's nostrils and woke him up, Joey headed to the kitchen where he selected a razor-sharp cutting knife. His father, Al Bonita, was out of town closing a sales conference and his little one-year-old sister, Tina, was having a hard time breathing because congestion from a chest cold.

Joey slid his mother's bedroom door open and walked in as if in a trance. Wol guided his hand as he drew the razor-sharp blade across his sister's windpipe. She was sleeping in a crib in the corner of the bedroom. He sent her instantly to eternity. Without thinking, he went over to his sleeping mother and stabbed her five times in the chest. He left the knife lying next to her, and then went back to sleep. In the morning he got up and went down to make himself breakfast. He went to his mother's room and found her in a pile of blood. He did what he had always been told to do in an emergency; he dialed 911 and waited for an ambulance.

Police had come along with the paramedics and immediately sealed off the scene to prevent any tampering with the evidence. Joey sat back playing with Star and watched as they took the gurney out with his mother and sister. A female police officer came over to talk with him and asked where his father was. She told him his mother was dead.

At first, none of them suspected him of having anything to do with it until Detective Robbie Mayer got on the scene and saw the small, bloody handprints on the knife and blood spattered all over Joey's pajamas. He called the juvenile authorities and had Joey taken in for questioning, although the only question that was in his mind was—WHY?

"This is the fourth time one of these kids with the Imps was in the paper," Wedge ranted. "It doesn't take a Ph.D. to see this is all connected. You're blowing it and if you keep making these mistakes, you're going to find yourself rotting in the desert. Now get the rest of these toys back and let's get out of here. This idea of test marketing was crazy. I should have never listened to you."

In truth, Wedge was the one who thought of it and it was Mia that objected, but now that it went wrong, he needed a scapegoat and Mia was the perfect one.

Mia knew that getting all the Imps back from the kids was going to be nearly impossible. There were 30 kids scattered all over the south side of Phoenix. Many of them lived in apartments, low-income housing, and were sure to put up a fight. Others didn't even have a clear-cut address, being shuffled between parents, aunts, uncles, grandparents, and nearly anyone who would take them. She decided the best thing to do was to go to the school and do a factory recall.

Lloyd Ziegler nearly ran into Mia on the way into the plain brick building. He looked at her and could sense that something was not right. She was accompanied by Wedge, who was wearing copper-colored, mirrored sunglasses and a black, loose-fitting silk suit.

"Excuse us," Mia offered. "We didn't mean to run you over."

Ziegler stepped aside and opened the door. "You folks looking for something? I'm Lloyd Ziegler, school psychologist."

"Yes, I'm Mia Tannersly, Tannersly Toys. To be quite honest, we are here to do a recall of our test project. Our engineer has detected a small leak in the power supply. We need to bring them in for replacement. Do you know where Mrs. Thompson's class is?"

"Yes, I do." Ziegler eyed them suspiciously. "But you need to check into the principal's office." He pointed down the hall. "Right down there."

Wedge was furious. He was hoping to walk into class unnoticed, take the toys, and disappear without a trace, just leaving everyone wondering. Now he would have to face the principal.

"Rahil, did I not tell you to make sure no one would spot us? That is an inexcusable slipup. He is surely one of the chosen," Santero demanded.

"Yes, Lord Santero, you did. I checked this place this morning. There was no trace of the Gods of War. Besides, how can I ever concentrate sharing this cursed body with Nefroties? My host grows uncomfortable with us here. I feel pangs and know that somewhere inside she is crying out to the Mighty One for deliverance."

"I'll deal with her after we get those toys back. I should have known never to put so much power in Lubato's hands. He is used to total subservience. He doesn't realize that here in America everything in the new media is based around sensationalism. If we don't get these toys back, our whole project will be a failure. I will stay and convince the principal. You go on to the classroom."

Mia went to classroom 15, where Mrs. Thompson was at the blackboard explaining the class reading assignment.

"Can anyone tell me what other name Mark Twain wrote under?" Mrs. Thompson asked. She looked up, startled to see Mia standing in back of her classroom, almost as if she had materialized under the door.

"Miss Tannersly," Mrs. Thompson said, looking at the class, "may I help you?"

"Yes, I'm very sorry for disturbing the class, but we have discovered a power supply leak in the Imps and we need to recall them for repair. Are they all here?"

She looked around at the nearly full class and saw most of them sitting on the students' desks.

"No, they aren't. Joey Bonita didn't come in today. His mother was found dead along with his little sister. They have him at juvenile hall." She put her hands on her hips as if to challenge Mia. "You sure there's not something wrong with these toys? A lot has been happening since you gave them to my class."

"No, not at all," Mia explained. "We should have them right back at the end of the week. Has anyone here learned anything from their Imp?"

Darius stood up. "My mom doesn't like my Imp. She thinks it's spooky. I like him. I named him Oogie." He sat down and said to Oogie, "Are you going to miss me, Oogie?"

"You bet I am, Darius, but I'll be back." Oogie craned his neck to look at Mia. "Isn't that right, Miss Tannersly?"

"Yes, Oogie, now I'd like everyone to bring their toys here to me. They are all tagged so we'll make sure you get the right one back."

The class got in line, marched their toys over, and put them on the desk in front of Mia. She took one look at all of them and began to grow dizzy from lack of oxygen. Before she could stop herself, she had fainted.

"Quit crowding me," Nefroties shouted at Rahil. "Stay on your own side of her."

"Well, she's no use to either of us now," Rahil responded. "Santero is planning on getting rid of her anyway. He considers her much too troublesome."

Wedge was surprised to see Mia unconscious rolling past him into a waiting ambulance. He took advantage of the confusion, walked in the classroom, and gathered up all the Imps, wondering where the 30th one was. He was happy that Mia was out of the way.

Several hours later, Bruce pulled up in front of the school in his Ford Escort Rent-a-Car and went in to see Lloyd, who was monitoring a study hall. Lloyd spotted him waving from the outside window. As Lloyd reached the hall, they embraced.

"You made it," Lloyd said. "Bring any strange diseases back from the Bay Area?"

"Yeah," Bruce joked, "I brought back a case of scitzotuma."

"Scitzotuma," Lloyd looked at him funnily, "what's that?"

"It's where one-half of you is up and the other half is down. I think I left part of my stomach up at 8,000 feet. The turbulence was really bad."

"Yeah, very funny. You were always a bust with the jokes, Bruce."

"Mia Tannersly was here this morning. She and some guy wearing a dark silk suit and sunglasses came to take away the Imps."

"Wedge Harwood," Bruce added. "I met him in the Bay Area. Sort of a creep."

"Bruce," Lloyd added, "he's more than a creep, he reeks evil. I can't explain how he made me feel. It's like I was totally dirty inside. I can hardly tell you how bad it feels even being close to him. It's like he can look right inside your soul and make you feel like you're hiding some horrible crime."

"That's the nature of Santero's attacks, Lloyd. In His own words, the Mighty One calls Santero the accuser of the brethren. His whole existence is focused on getting us to look at our own faults and not at the Mighty One for His forgiveness. Back before I accepted the Mighty One's forgiveness for my sins, I was involved in smuggling drugs from Mexico. Several times I sold them to children under 18. After I repented and accepted the Mighty One's forgiveness, I would still be haunted by guilt for what I had done."

"How did you deal with it?"

"I couldn't handle it. I prayed about it and finally it all passed away. Every time the feeling of guilt came, I realized I was being spiritually attacked. I still go through it now. It's not something that ever stops either. Your own conscience bothers you. Do you have one of the Imps here that I can see?"

"No, in the confusion of Mia Tannersly being taken out to the ambulance after passing out, her associate collected all of them except the one belonging to Joey Bonita. His is probably at his house, but it's not going to be easy getting it."

"Why? What happened?"

"This morning, while his father was away on business, Joey slit his sister's throat and stabbed his mother. They have him at the juvenile holding center, and I don't think his dad will talk to anyone."

"I'd like to try anyway. I want to see if it's possible for us to get our hands on that Imp. If it really is behind everything, it's gonna take some doing to keep these things from landing in the states."

"Look, Bruce, I haven't talked to you since I talked to Darius Mendez. I tricked his Imp into divulging who he really was. He called himself Lubato, ruler of the small ones, formerly from the Far East. Darius named him Oogie, but that sure wasn't what he called himself."

"Sounds wild, but I've had run-ins before with spirits. Do you know where they took Mia Tannersly? I feel like we should go and visit her after we see the kid's father."

It felt good to Bruce to back on his home turf. All the driving up and down the hills of the Bay Area made him appreciate how easy it was getting around in a town like Phoenix where everything stayed pretty flat. They hopped on the new Papago Freeway, decorated with huge pots, and headed into Paradise Valley to the juvenile facility where they were holding Joey. They figured they would find his father there.

The juvenile holding center was on the corner of Thunderbird and 32nd Street next to Chompie's Bagel Nosh, where they stopped to formulate their strategy and pick up some onion bagels and cream cheese. Their throats were parched from the heat.

"I'm a little nervous," Lloyd confided. "This is beyond my job description, visiting kids that murder their parents."

"You want to get to the bottom of this, don't you?" Bruce queried. "Then we've got to get the toy. If we don't, we'll never find out."

"How can you expect to find out whether or not a toy is demon possessed?" Lloyd took another sip of his Mountain Dew and stirred his ice with a straw.

"I don't know, but if this is really happening, then I'm sure the Mighty One has a strategy. I'm just glad I spent the morning praying. If these things are controlled by the fallen, it's going to take a lot of help from the warriors to counteract what they've already done."

Lloyd flashed his credentials and the County Sheriff let him in the holding room where they brought in Joey Bonita. He was only 11 and couldn't have weighed more than 85 pounds. He had a mop of pitch-black, thick hair. His deep brown eyes revealed his Italian heritage. He was escorted by a female officer.

"You've got 30 minutes, Doc," she recited as by rote, not even glancing at Bruce. "If you need to talk with his parent, he's in the other room with the kid's lawyer, although I'll warn you, the dad's a mess."

Lloyd stood. "Sit down, Joey." He indicated where he wanted Joey to sit. "I brought along a friend that wants to help you. This is Reverend Bruce."

"Just call me Bruce," Bruce said, putting his hand on Joey's shoulder and helping him find his seat. "Do you know really why you're in here?"

"They told me my mom and sister were dead and they thought that I did it," he said, choking back tears. "Why would I do something like that? I love my mom. I love my little sister."

"Any idea what happened?" Lloyd asked. "Any at all?"

"They told me my fingerprints were on the knife, but I don't remember doing anything to either of them. I couldn't have killed them. Really, I couldn't have. I found blood all over my mom's bed and I called 911 like I have always been taught. My dad was traveling for his job." Joey broke down in tears.

Bruce went over to Lloyd. "Whatever happened, the kid has a mental block."

"Joey, tell us about your new toy Imp," Lloyd asked.

"I named him Star. He's really cool. He says hi when I come home from school, knows what my favorite foods are, and can even smell them. When I ride him home on my bike, he can even tell me the types and years of the cars. He even helps me with my homework."

"Think back, Joey." Bruce leaned in closer to him, putting both of his hands on Joey's shoulders. "Did Star tell you to hurt your mom and sister?"

Joey stopped and reflected on what Bruce was asking. "It did really bother me that Tina was crying. I had a dream about knives but I don't remember Star telling me anything."

"Do you turn Star off at night before you go to sleep?"

"No, the lady said we didn't have to, that the battery would last for years. We could just leave them on and have them wake us up. What does Star have to do with this?"

"Where is Star now?" Bruce asked directly.

"I hid him after I called 911," Joey responded. "He told me to hide him and I did."

"Where?" Lloyd asked.

"I built my own tree house last summer with my dad. I hid him in that."

"What's your address?" Lloyd asked.

"718 East Jones," Joey replied. He looked as if he had betrayed someone. "I feel guilty telling you. I promised Star I'd hide him."

Bruce put his hand reassuringly on Joey's shoulder. "You did the right thing telling us. Rest assured, we'll take good care of Star."

"Can you bring him in to see me?" Joey asked. "Everyone else seems so mad at me like I did it."

"I don't think the police will let us bring him in, but we'll tell him you said hello."

At that moment,t he door opened up and a big, burly fellow with hands the size of a catcher's mit walked in accompanied by Lieutenant Robbie Mayer. Joey jumped up and ran over.

"Dad," he cried, clinging on to his enormous waist. "I didn't mean to do anything. Really, I didn't." Joey looked up to get his father's approval.

His father, teary eyed, put his huge hands on top of Joey's head and fought back the tears. "I know, son. Everything will be all right."

Lloyd stuck out his hand to meet Mr. Bonita. "I'm Lloyd Ziegler, the counselor at Joey's school. This is Reverend Bruce. I brought him along for some advice."

Robbie stepped up. "I hardly think this is a spiritual matter. The evidence is pretty clear cut."

Maybe the evidence," Bruce responded, "but what of the motive?"

Robbie stepped forward to interrupt. "Motive—that's for the prosecutor to decide. The young man's prints are on the murder weapon."

"Doesn't it seem at all odd to you that so many of the children from that class have been linked to violent crimes after showing no previous signs?" Lloyd questioned. "It certainly does to me."

Mr. Bonita straightened up. "If you two don't mind, this is my visiting time. I'd like some time alone with my son."

As Bruce and Lloyd drove down Central Avenue past boarded-up buildings, vacant lots, and untended palm trees that were havens for the neighborhood pigeons, they saw the big orange barriers that read: DRUG FREE NEIGHBORHOOD that made turning on Jones Street difficult. They pulled up in front of the house and walked around to the backyard where they saw the tree house.

"Give me a hand getting up this tree," Bruce said. "I don't think I'm dressed for tree climbing."

"If you don't want to," Lloyd volunteered, smiling, "I'll go up. Just give the word. I'm not too old."

Star was switched off when Bruce took him down from the tree. Joey had stashed him in one of his father's old aluminum lunch buckets. They activated him and he began to speak.

"Hi, I'm Star," the toy spoke.

"Hi, Star, tell me," Lloyd asked, "have you always been Star or did you have another life before now?"

"Why do you ask? What is the importance of your question?"

"I command you to come out," Bruce spoke with authority. "Whatever spirit is in there, identify yourself and come out. In the name of all that is holy, the raised spirit of the Mighty One, Lord Immortal Yeshua Ha Machia."

The robot began to vibrate and grew hot in Lloyd's hands. The head moved back and forth as if it wasn't even connected with the body. Smoke began to emit from the robot's microprocessor sections as the soldering connections heated up.

"My name is Wol. I am the spirit of the departed, the sacred one of the guardians of the Great Wall. Leave me be. What have you with me?"

It was you who directed Joey to murder his mother and sister, wasn't it?" Bruce queried. "We bind you on earth as you are bound in heaven. We subject you to the laws of the Mighty One who has given us His followers all dominion and authority. We bind you to spend the remainder of your time until judgement cast into the pit that the Mighty One prepared for all who rebelled and sinned against Him."

Yoballa met the spirit inside of Star and challenged him, his sword drawn and dazzling, with an eternal brightness that blinded Wol.

"You have been commanded by my charge to leave. I must bind you as well, Wol." Yoballa looked at him with compassion. "It was you who chose to rebel. Had you stayed, we would not be enemies; we would be friends."

Wol knew it was hopeless to struggle against the light bands. They seared his body, reminding him of the light that flowed from the presence of the Mighty One. He fell unconscious and felt himself being transported to the very bowels of the earth. The subterranean cavity grew darker and he could smell the limestone and sulphur as the core of Planet Earth, a molten lava ocean, sloshed and spewed forth temperatures beyond imagination. He knew that the pain he would experience for eternity would be immense. He knew being separated from the love of the Mighty One was to be in eternal torment, never getting a moment of peace or release, always tormented without thoughts of why and second guessing himself as to why he had ever allowed himself to be drawn to Santero.

It all seemed so innocent at first. Santero had addressed a number of the small ones and complained of the new beings that the Mighty One was planning on creating and how they would probably be loved more, and the Mighty One wouldn't have time for the other guardians and small ones. To Wol's mind, it seemed quite illogical, but he received what Santero said and began to mull it over. When Santero addressed a group of them and told how he alone would always love them and that they must act to remove the Mighty One from power before He could bring about the changes He was planning, Wol found himself being swept along in the hysteria. They overthrew Gund, the leader of the small ones, and descended on the very throne of the Mighty One to remove Him from the Circle of Light. The battle went on for what seemed an eternity. Michael the Guardian fought off the last wave of attackers, relentlessly dispersing Santero and all that had followed him to the Planet Earth. In his rage, Santero began reeking havoc on Planet Earth, trying to prevent the Mighty One's creation of humans.

Wol was swept along with the other fallen, nursing his wounds and wondering why he had picked the losing side. He tried to make the best of a bad situation, but was unable to even come to peace with his decision.

He landed with a thud in a blackened pit and knew instantly that until the final day of judgment, he was sealed in isolation. He tried to remember some of the songs they had sung around the Mighty One's throne but his mind drew a blank. He was so filled with evil that good, wholesome thought could no longer exist in his mind.

* * * * *

Mia lay in her hospital room at John C. Lincoln Hospital, looking out at the Squaw Peak Mountains. She drifted in and out of consciousness and thought back to a sermon about Christ that she heard at a Chinese church in San Francisco while she was still a college student. She remembered the minister had talked about the time that the Son of the Mighty One had cast demons out of a crazy man and the demons had gone into a nearby herd of swine that went berserk and drowned themselves. She wished she could drown herself. She didn't know exactly how many spirits had inhabited her, but she knew there were many. She pushed the buzzer, and when the nurse came in, managed to ask for a glass of orange juice. Her body temperature was approaching 110 and they had packed ice on both sides of her, trying to cool her down. They drew blood samples, but could not determine exactly what it was that was causing the fever. The doctor and lab techs were baffled.

* * * * *

"The Mighty One warned all of us not to listen to Santero when he was Lucifer, star of the morning. You ignored the warning and allowed yourself to be seduced. Now look at where it has brought you, destroying the very lives that your Creator made—souls unlike ourselves with the power of free choice."

"Is there no chance for me, Yoballa?" Wol pleaded. "No chance to accompany you back to the Circle of Light and be restored? I am sorry for the choice I made. I loathe Santero. He is the ultimate liar and rules over us with terror and fear. I hate who I have become. I miss the love the Mighty One. Please."

Yoballa removed the light band and left Wol in the deep pit. "I wish you could be forgiven, for I see that you are truly distraught at what you have become. But for us, there is no cleaning, no regeneration. We lived in the presence of the Mighty One for so many eons, experienced His love, kindness, goodness, lived and dwelled in His light, and even after that, you turned to darkness. There is no return. You have chosen the path that leads to an eternal separation. Although my heart is filled with the joy of one who dwells continually with the Mighty One, I regret that you can no longer experience His presence as I do. Now you must wait, as many of the others do, for that day of judgment where you will be sentenced. It is beyond my power and authority to decide your fate."

CHAPTER FOURTEEN

THE FURY, THE POWER, THE GLORY

Wedge Harwood grabbed the America West non-stop to San Jose and checked in the Imps in a large trunk which he had purchased from Abba's Antiques in Tempe on the way to the airport. He had carelessly thrown the Imps in the trunk and was more concerned with getting back to San Jose to make sure the shipment of 100,000, all pre-sold, got into the country without incident. He smiled as the plane took off from Sky Harbor Airport and headed over the vast wasteland that separated Phoenix from the Bay Area. As he glanced down, he wished that he could once again reduce the earth to a vast wasteland without human habitation—a wasteland where he and the fallen could live without being bothered by the Mighty One and the guardians. He longed for the day when he could fight the Mighty One on His own turf and bring Him groveling before his feet. He knew it was predicted by the Mighty One in His Word to men, but he believed that the Mighty One falsely predicted victory, and that instead of the Great Santero, Deceiver of the Nations ending up in chains cast into the Lake of Fire at the center of the earth, it would be the Mighty One who would be cast down and forced to create another existence for Himself beyond the known universe. He smiled perversely at the thought and looked up when the stewardess asked him for his drink order.

"I'll have a Bloody Mary," he replied, wishing it was her blood he could drink.

"That will be three dollars," the young flight attendant responded.

Wedge handed her the money and watched her go on to the next aisle. The fury within him grew and he began to hate humans more and more. Santero had totally dominated Wedge's spirit, and outside of Wedge's original mannerisms in speech and physical movement, he was just a shell that Santero controlled every moment.

* * * * *

The container ship built by Hyundai of Korea left the harbor at Hong Kong loaded with every kind of export bound for the United States. Two 40-foot containers numbered and marked were headed for the docks in Long Beach where they would be shipped to distribution centers through the United States. Each of the containers held 50,000 Imps, all with subterranean creatures dwelling in them. The darkness of the container was not uncomfortable to the small ones who had spent nearly 40 years locked below the Shou Lin Temple. They were anxious to arrive in America and fulfill the wishes of their leader, Santero. It was a job they had grown to relish.

On Tuesday, when Brian went to work, he ran into Wedge Harwood pushing the old trunk towards the main conference room.

"Good morning, Wedge," Brian said cheerfully. "Can I give you a hand? The trunk looks kind of awkward. My dad had one like that. He inherited it from my grandfather."

"No, don't need any help. These are the test toys from Phoenix."

"You pulled them from the test?"

"Yeah," Wedge said, challenging Brian, "they worked well and we pulled them. I know you got the new microprocessors done and I'd like you to rig these up with the new guts. No problem, right?"

Wedge tried to back Brian into the wall. Brian sidestepped him. "No, of course not. Where's Mia?"

"She's in the hospital in Phoenix. They have her in for tests. I've got some buyers coming from Wal-Mart. It's the one chain we haven't closed. Can you get these ready by tomorrow morning?"

"I've got a term paper I'm working on. It's midterm." Brian stared at the hatred in Wedge's eyes. "But why not just wheel them into the lab and I'll grab a few technicians and get right to work. I'll have them for you, Wedge. Don't you worry one bit."

Brian darted into his office where he hooked up the computer and dialed home to talk with Alice.

She answered the phone breathless, having exercised with a fit and fitness show. "Hi," she said.

"Alice, Wedge is acting really weird. He said Mia is in the hospital down in Phoenix. Didn't Bruce say he was going down there?"

"Yeah, he's down there right now. What do you mean, weird?"

"His eyes, they're like red . . ."

"Look, just stay out of his way," Alice pondered. "Maybe I should check out really what's happening to Mia. I can call the church and find out where Bruce is at. It's only a one-hour flight."

"Good idea. If these things . . ." Brian choked. "If there is something weird happening, I'm going to blow the lid off this whole stew."

"I'll call you and let you know where I'm going to be."

Alice got on the phone with Denise Hauser and found out where Bruce was staying. She managed to get him on the phone at the Hyatt Regency Gainey Ranch.

"Bruce," Alice spoke, "it's me, Alice Phillips, from the church. Brian just called me from Tannersly. He said Wedge Harwood really has wigged out. He told him Mia was in the hospital. Have you seen her?"

"No, but we got ahold of one of the Imps. There's something strange happening with them. Can Brian come down?"

"He's got to do some work. Maybe I should come down and see for myself. Brian wants to blow the lid on the whole project. Can you get a room there for me? I'm going to need to be picked up from the airport too. They won't rent me a car. I'm too young. I'll be flying in if I can make it on America West #452. It should be in around 1:30."

"No problem, I'll be down at the baggage. I'll see you then."

Ballelulia knew a confrontation was coming. He felt recharged as Alice prayed for strength and Denise from the Alliance Christian Center got a prayer chain going.

* * * * *

Brian knew he might have to activate the virus and trigger the cybernet to lock up the electrical system on the Imp. He punched up the screen and entered his ten-digit code to review what he would have to do. He had already figured out Mia's entry code and was able to enter it and find the container line, date, and port of entry. He made a mental note. He knew that to trigger the virus he would need an amplifier capable of broadcasting loud enough to resonate through the container walls of thick half-inch steel. He wasn't sure how much power he would need and decided he needed to test it. The only problem was getting an Imp out from under Wedge's nose. He knew he would have to come back that night when the lab was closed and somehow get out with one of the Imps and have it back early the next morning. While he was pondering the situation, the phone rang.

"Brian," Alice said, "I'm going down to Phoenix. I'll be staying in Scottsdale at the Hyatt at Gainey Ranch. Why don't you come with me?"

"I'd love to, really, but believe me, now is not the time. Some heavy stuff is going down around here. Call me when you get there."

* * * * *

Bruce was there to pick Alice up. She had worn a denim outfit with sequins, looking more like a rock star's girlfriend than anything else. Bruce was conservatively dressed in a light blue shirt and khaki pants with topsiders. He took her back to the school where Lloyd was waiting with the Imp.

They hurried down the hallway to the science lab, which was deserted except for Lloyd and the Imp.

"Who's that?" the Imp questioned.

"I'm Alice," she said. "Who are you?"

"Don't worry about it," Lloyd said. "Whatever spirits were in it are not there anymore."

"How can you be sure?" Alice questioned. "Really, how do you know?"

"We cast it out. You could feel it leave the room. The machine like sputtered and gave off some smoke. It was like a scene from the Exorcist," Bruce spoke with authority. "I think what we need to do now is get in to see Mia. I'm friends with a chaplain who works at that hospital and I'm sure we can get clearance. We should spend the afternoon in prayer because whatever has got hold of her is not going to let go easily."

Bruce, Lloyd, and Alice dropped to their knees right in the science room. They began to speak in heavenly languages and intercede to the Mighty One on behalf of Mia. As they all prayed for her, Alice saw a vision of the two fallen battling for control of her. She stopped her prayer to speak about it.

"I see this vision of a giant wolf-like creature and also a very seductive spirit battling for control. I see Mia. She is like a prisoner in her own body. She is screaming for help but seems unable to get out the words. It's like a silent scream," Alice said, as if mesmerized by the dream. "I've never had a vision like this before."

"God is showing us what we are dealing with. Who knows how many other spirits have entered her as well. They love to possess human bodies and manipulate them," Bruce said.

* * * * *

Mia, although still quite unconscious, had been clawing herself and drooling. The nurse caught her lacerating her chest and they ordered restraints for her. No one quite understood what was happening to her and they had no next of kin to call and no one from Tannersly had even inquired about her.

By the time Bruce, Lloyd, and Alice arrived at the hospital, it was 6:00 p.m. and the hallway was pretty much deserted. They signed in and went down to her room. The television was on but her roommate was out in the lobby visiting with friends. Bruce went and examined the bandages on her.

"Mia," Bruce exclaimed as he put his hand on her forehead. "She must be 110 degrees. She's burning up!"

Lloyd went around to the other side. "She sure is."

Alice went and opened her eyelid. A soft glow of red emanated from her eye. Alice jumped back when she saw the reflection of Rahil, the wolflike demon being. "Bruce, in here." She held an eyelid up as Bruce came to take a look. "Do you see it? There, in that red glow."

"Wow, I do." Bruce stepped back and watched Mia's body begin to shake.

A voice emanated from her. It was deep and foreign, yet it moved her tongue. "Cursed followers of the Mighty One. I am Rahil, destroyer of all goodness. Be gone." Her eyes opened and they looked right at Alice. "Where is your beer and wine, young one, and your Seven and Sevens? Surely you don't think you have the power to cast me out." Rahil glanced at Lloyd and roared, "And you with your pornographic novels in the interest of psychology. You surely don't have the power." He looked at Bruce, "You with your secret desires for sex. You really think you have the power to cast me forth?"

"Bruce," Lloyd spoke, "don't listen to him. He's trying to get us to focus on ourselves and not the power of the Mighty One."

"It's true," Alice said, "I used to drink, but now . . ."

She was interrupted by another voice. "Yes, now you no longer drink, but you still consult your chart everyday, don't you? I know much about charts. I used to read them for the Pharaoh. You pathetic humans leave us be. This one is ours. This host suits our purposes fine."

"You're burning her up," Bruce spoke with authority. "Loose her spirits in the name of the Mighty One and His immortal Son who defeated you on the cross. The Lord of Heaven and the Earth. Be gone."

A deep laugh came from Mia's chest. "You think to fool us with that be gone, you be gone. We are here to stay."

"We?" Alice asked. "How many are you?"

The voices began to come out of her. "We are legion."

From her mouth, dark spirits began to come forth piercing the room into darkness and oppressing the three visitors. Alice, Bruce, and Lloyd joined hands and began to pray out loud in the spirit. The window began to rattle and they watched in horror as Mia's frail body was slammed up and down on the bed and began to float about the room.

* * * * *

"Loose her," Ballelulia spoke. "Rahil, come forth and face me. Don't hide like a coward."

Rahil materialized in back of Ballelulia and slashed him across the back. "You turn and face me, great warrior," Rahil spit out.

Yoballa materialized in the midst of the swirling spirits. "Don't you think two of us is more of a fair fight?" Yoballa challenged lassoing Rahil's arm with his light band. "It works better for us when the odds are a little more even."

"Cursed guardian," Rahil shuddered with pain while gripping his paw. "Can you do nothing fair?"

Nefroties rose next to Rahil, accompanied by Marmorphis. They spoke in unison.

"Don't forget us." They attacked Yoballa who sidestepped both of their thrusts and sent them sprawling while Ballelulia edged up to his back, holding two swords.

Ballelulia said, "How many more of you are there? Come out of here in the name of the Most High. We serve you notice that your judgment day is nigh."

They looked and found themselves surrounded by over 50 demonic beings who rushed at them tearing at their hands and feet. One after another, the attackers came, some on all fours, some flying, spewing forth flames and foul smells. Ballelulia and Yoballa withstood wave after wave of them swinging their swords as if they were threshing wheat. They bound those who got close enough with their light bands until there was just Nefroties and Rahil standing.

"Now the odds are even," Yoballa spoke as Rahil back up and tried to vaporize back into Mia's mouth. Before he could vaporize, the light bands were around his feet. "No, you don't. We're sending you into a cave on the outer darkness to await your judgment."

"You, Nefroties," Ballelulia entreated. "Will you come quietly or shall we maim you? My sword can cripple you for eternity."

"No, you have won. Against all odds you have triumphed." Nefroties extended his hands. "Bind me if you must, but not too tightly. The light of the Mighty One still casts a searing pain in my soul because I realize that I never should have rebelled against Him."

Ballelulia and Yoballa strung them all together and pulled them out of the room. They took them to the center of the earth where they sealed them all in a cave to wait for their doom.

* * * * *

The room grew light and Bruce, Lloyd, and Alice opened their eyes.

"They're gone," Bruce said. "I'm sure our guardians won. Our prayers have been answered. Can you feel the difference? Look, Mia is stirring."

Mia struggled to get up. "Where am I? Why are these bonds on me?" She looked over at Alice. "I know you. You're Brian Phillips's wife. Where am I?"

Alice went over to her and held her hand, trying to calm her down. "You don't remember anything?"

Mia looked at the bandages covering her. "What happened to me? Why am I covered with bandages?"

"You were trying to scratch yourself. Mia, this may seem hard to believe, but you were filled with evil spirits. Some of the fallen had taken residence in your body. They were controlling you," Bruce stated.

"I can vaguely remember. I felt like I was drowning but it was so hot, I couldn't breath. My head seemed full of smoke. Then all of a sudden there was this light and I woke up."

"The light was the light of the Mighty One whose son Jesus Christ set you free from the evil ones. You need to accept Him in your life now or the fallen will return and it will be seven times worse," Bruce cautioned. "Your body has been swept clean, but if they return and you're not full of the spirit of the Almighty, it will be worse."

"How do I get full of the spirit?" Mia asked. "I mean, what am I supposed to do? I would really be crazy to want the fallen back living in me. I've had a battle going inside of me. Everything seemed so smoky and I couldn't breathe."

"Do you know anything of the Mighty One's son, Jesus Christ?" Bruce asked.

"Yeah, a little. I heard different things. My dad belonged to the Church of England."

"Do you believe He died for your sins and rose from the grave?"

"Yeah, I don't see why that would be so hard to believe. After all, his tomb is still empty and people come back from the dead even now. I mean, gosh, I just came back from the dead, so to speak."

"Hold my hand. Let us lead you in a prayer that will seal your spirit from possession by the fallen."

As Bruce led her in prayer, Alice and Lloyd gathered around and called on the Mighty One to infuse her with the spirit of the risen one. A soft glow began to come on her countenance as she felt the all-powering love of the ages fill her very innermost being. She was so full of joy that she began to cry and utter languages unknown to her. She lifted her arms up. Alice joined her in praise and began to sing softly in a heavenly tongue. Miraculously, none of the nurses disturbed them and an hour later, they stopped praying, knowing that they had been visited by the Mighty One Himself.

* * * * *

Santero grew restless as Wedge's physical health deteriorated from lack of sleep, exercise, and constant movement. The exterior shell began to resemble a walking zombie as it paced the halls of Tannersly Industries, gloating over his grand scheme to destroy so many innocent lives.

Brian was diligently at work installing the ungraded chips in time for the meeting with Walmart. He didn't dare risk any more phone calls. He was determined to leave the minute he was done and then return later that evening.

When he wrapped up his work, he placed the Imp in a box. He put the box on a cart and rolled it down the hallway. He heard pacing outside of Wedge's door and looked in. He was shocked to see Wedge banging his head on the small walnut conference table. Wedge looked up and rushed toward the door, throwing it open. Brian reacted in shock, reeling backward, away from the door.

"They're done," Brian said. "I was just delivering them."

"If they're done," Wedge smiled, "then you're done. I think you know too much and have seen too much."

Brian walked backward, away from Wedge's menacing approach. "What do you mean, I've seen too much? I did just what you asked me to do. I installed the new microprocessor, and they work fine."

"You know what I mean. You're not dumb, Brian Phillips. You know these are not merely toys, don't you? You know these Imps are meant for far more than that." Wedge nearly had him backed into a corner and Brian darted out from under his outstretched arms.

Brian made a run for the exit door with Wedge clambering behind. It was locked. He panicked and looked at his watch. 10:00 p.m. He muttered a curse at himself for staying so late. He knew no one would be in until 7:00 the next morning. He rushed down the hall into the men's room and hid in a stall where he sat on the back of the toilet and hoped not to be discovered.

Wedge looked for him for about an hour and stopped after finding no trace of him. Santero left Wedge's body sprawled across the conference table. He traveled through another dimension to supervise the placement of the Imps.

* * * * *

Cadaver, Sawtooth, Matush, Maduke, and a hoard of other fallen were called to the pit by Santero to discuss the protection of the Imps.

Sawtooth nervously pranced back and forth, limping severely. "Lord Santero, do any other of the Mighty One's followers know about the shipment?"

"You think me a fool, Sawtooth? No one knows of the shipment except Mia Tannersly and my host. She is flat on her back in a hospital and won't be telling anyone," Santero said proudly. "Cadaver, I want you to make sure nothing happens to the container when it lands in Long Beach—and take Maduke with you. Don't leave the container until the contents have been safely transferred to the distribution center in Corona."

"Yes, Lord Santero," Cadaver replied, wondering what would go wrong with Santero's new scheme after seeing so many in the past go amiss at the last moment.

"Lord Santero," Cadaver said as he rose from the limestone he was seated on, "perhaps if you'd let me, I could supervise our forces and gather them before the container ship even arrives."

"Yes," Santero smiled, always grateful for Cadaver's suggestions. "Take a legion out to sea and guide the container ship in. Make sure it's not tampered with."

* * * * *

Louie Columbo had worked on the docks for about 18 years. He operated a huge crane that removed the containers from inside the ships and set them on the ground. Everyone knew him and everyone left him alone. His uncle was the former Joey Columbo from La Costra Nostra in New York City, who had been gunned down years earlier. Louie had his pick of incoming merchandise and nobody disputed that with him. Everyone knew about his scheme and were in on the take. If Mitsubishi sent over a container of 700 wide-screen television sets, 50 were gone before they ever hit the distribution center. When Sharp imported 3,000 VCRs, at least 200 or so disappeared while the container was waiting to clear Customs. Nobody ever knew anything, and those that were inclined to talk, knew from example that they'd end up with the fish if they did.

The container ship arrived without fanfare. It was one of many that used the huge Long Beach Harbor, bringing foreign goods of every description. Louie didn't have any children but knew there was a huge black market in children's toys and they were very easy to unload. When he saw the shipping manifest that listed over 100,000 of them, he knew he could make a good score.

* * * * *

Brian was still huddled on the toilet when the lights to the bathroom came on. He heard the sound of toilets flushing and someone tried to open his stall. He looked down and saw a pair of Nike sneakers and jeans and knew it wasn't Wedge. He sheepishly opened the door. It was a young kid of about 21.

"What are you doing here?" Brian asked.

"I'm the night janitor, Wes Holmbrook. What are you doing? Do you have diarrhea or something? Don't you know it's midnight? How can you see in the dark anyway?"

"Shhhhh," Brian said, putting his index finger to his mouth. "Have you got a key to the front?"

"No, no keys. We come in from the warehouse door and use our entry code from there. You look like you've seen something fierce."

"I have," Brian said. "Who else is here with you?"

"The foreman, Ted Williams, and Mario and Nick."

"Get them all together and tell them to get out now. Wedge Harwood, one of the directors, has gone crazy. I'm in here because he tried to kill me."

"Really?" Wes responded, his eyes opening wide. "You're really serious, aren't you?"

"Sure am. Just get out of here now."

Brian took off hoping that the janitors would get out safely. He knew that Wedge was really after him. He reasoned that with the shipment docking at 7:00 the next morning, he couldn't chance taking the morning plane. He headed home to pick up his portable generator and amplifier as well as a small synthesizer he had made with a variable pitch oscillator. By the time he packed them all in his Stealth, it was pretty crowded. He placed a call to Alice, but changed his mind when the desk clerk asked him if he was sure he wanted to disturb her. He opted to leave her a message with his destination. He drove inland where he picked up Interstate 5 and stepped on it. He knew that when the ship docked, it would be the last time all 100,000 of the Imps would be together at the same time. He was mad at himself for never doing a test through a steel box. He hoped his tones would be audible to the viruses planted inside the computers.

Alice woke up at 4:00 a.m. in a sweat. She looked over restlessly, glancing at the clock, and noticed the message light blinking. She got a glass of water, dialed the front desk, and picked up Brian's message. She figured she would try him on his car phone and managed to get him as he was heading through Bakersfield.

"Hello," Brian answered, slowing down so he could concentrate on the phone conversation. "What are you doing up in the middle of the night?" Couldn't sleep without me?"

"I can never sleep without you," Alice said. "Where are you?"

"Let's see, I'm passing a Wendy's, Taco Bell, and Roadway Inn," Brian said smartly.

"I mean what city?"

"I'm in Bakersfield, about an hour and a half from where I'm heading. If I make good time, I might miss the morning L.A. rush hour. How did it go down there? Sorry I couldn't call you earlier, but Wedge tried to kill me. At least, I thought he was trying. I didn't let him get close enough to find out."

"Kill you? What is happening? And why are going to L.A. in the middle of the night and driving? You must be exhausted!"

"I am, but I took some brain pills. I'm wide awake. In fact, I've really gotten to be a country music fan. That's all they play in the middle of the night and I forgot to pack my compact disks."

"Brian, please be serious. Why are you going to L.A.?"

"I'm going to trigger the virus and destroy these Imps. There's something drastically wrong with them. They're like little Chucky dolls, only they're real."

"Brian, you don't know who you're messing with. You shouldn't try this by yourself. I went through it tonight with Bruce and Lloyd. We cast some of these fallen spirits out of Mia and the whole room turned black. Please wait for us before you go in there. We can take a plane out and be there by seven o'clock. They leave every hour. Please, Brian, these things are too much for you. They're from another dimension and you can't fight them with natural means."

"You saying I don't have what it takes to beat these little critters? Alice, I helped design them," Brian said, getting perturbed.

"No, I know you're smart enough. It's just that there is something else living inside all of them. They aren't what you made. They're just using the shell—the Imps—to control children and incite them to violence."

"You sure you can get in at 7:00?" Brian asked.

"Yeah, I'll wake up Bruce now," Alice spoke. "I love you, Brian. We'll call you when we land. I'm going to go now, honey. I love you."

"I love you too, Alice. My little Alice in Wonderland. Hey, maybe when we finish this crazy adventure, you'll let me take you to Disneyland, okay?"

"Yeah, I'd love to go. Well, I'd better get Bruce. See you soon."

Alice hung up the phone. She went next door and pounded on Bruce's door. He answered the door with his t-shirt askew and his hair looked as if he had stuck his hand in an electrical circuit.

"Alice, what's up?" Bruce asked, trying to wipe the sleep out of his eyes. "Do you know what time it is?"

"Yeah, I do, but we've got to be out of here in an hour and a half. Brian's on his way to L.A. He's going to send his virus to dismantle the Imps. We'd better get over there and offer some support if the battle is anything like it was over Mia."

"You're right," Bruce said. "Who need sleep anyway? I'll call and make reservations on the six o'clock Southwest flight. How I ever got into this thing is beyond me."

"Maybe you were just in the right place at the right time," Alice smiled. "I was going to try and get some more sleep, but I can't even think about sleep."

* * * * *

Louis Columbo started his shift at midnight and got off at 8:00 a.m. The boat from Hong Kong docked at 4:00 a.m. and he looked at the manifest and had the crane out for the container from Tannersly Industries first. Pat Monday, his sister's husband, pulled a truck up to the pier and parked in back. The container was sealed and bonded, but neither one of them cared. A thousand or so of the new toys would net them each at least five grand. Their customers had learned never to ask questions—just accept the deals and pay cash. What they didn't know, they figured would never hurt them, and their Swap Mart buyers disposed of them before anyone even knew what was missing.

Columbo had a pair of large pipe cutters that were perfect for cutting container locks. He felt uneasy as he approached the large orange container and swore he heard voices coming from inside. As he reached up with the cutters to cut the lock, he heard footsteps and felt a shadow pass over him. It chilled him deep within. He lifted the cutters to the lock and everything broke loose. The container rocked on its own, and as he jumped back in shock, he fell on the cutters which, due to his strange angle, pierced his kidneys. His brother-in-law came running.

"Louie!" Pat yelled as he gathered over him, unsure of what to do or who to call.

"Pat," Louie said, struggling for air. "Pull them out. I can't breathe."

Pat rolled Louie over and saw the cutters poking through his back. He pulled them out, sending forth a huge stream of blood and bits of flesh. He attempted to stop the flow of blood with his own jacket, but it was hopeless. Less than two minutes went by and Louie lay dead in his arms. Pat moved him into the truck and drove away, wondering how he would ever explain what had happened.

Sawtooth grinned in glee. A little push and shove and one more stupid human entered eternity without knowing the Mighty One and without being forgiven of their sins. He marveled at how really crazy most humans were for trading paradise for earthly treasures and pleasures, none of which ever truly satisfied them.

Cadaver watched as the truck pulled away with Louie. He turned to Maduke. "No one disturbs these," he spoke threateningly. "If they do, they die just like this one."

CHAPTER FIFTEEN

SHOWDOWN

Brian fumbled with the city map at the AmPm market on Century Boulevard, just down the street from the International Airport. It took him a while to look up the code and locate the Long Beach docks and then find a good route there. It was 6:00 a.m. He had made good time, but knew that the shipment could be almost anywhere. He got mad at himself for forgetting to bring binoculars and then remembered that Louie's eyesight was terrific. He was glad he had designed Louie and wished he had never had anything to do with the Imps. He walked in the market and got himself a cup of coffee. He walked to the counter to pay for it.

"Looks like you had a rough night," the sales clerk addressed him.

"Yeah," Brian said, reaching in his wallet. "Here, keep the change."

"Thanks." The sales clerk looked and pointed to his cross. "It's none of my business but I'm a follower of the Mighty One. I saw you coming in here, sort of a vision type thing. I'll be praying for you. I don't know what it is you're supposed to be doing, but whatever it is, the Mighty One wants you to know he's with you all the way. He'll send his warriors to guard you."

Los Angeles had been known as the City of Angels. If anyone could have seen into the hidden dimension, they would have seen the tremendous influx of the fallen as they gathered around the containers. There were at least three legions of them of every description. The men who worked in the shipyard found themselves irritated and cursing one another. The sky overhead was unusually murky even for a city known worldwide for its constant smog.

The Chief Warrior of the city, Ahtel, was worried to see so many of the fallen descending on his territory like swarms of locusts. He knew they were only there to steal, kill, and destroy and wondered how to stop them. He left Archangel Gothos in charge and traveled to visit the Mighty One.

As he grew near the Circle of Light, he was refreshed beyond measure. The wounds and battle weariness that he felt from continually shouldering the messages and burdens of the followers were healed. He stopped by the crystal river to take a drink and proceeded to the throne of the Mighty One.

"Greeting, Warrior Ahtel," the Mighty One thundered. "No doubt you are concerned about events in your city. I too bear your concern, so you do not stand alone, Warrior. I stand with you."

"Praise and honor unto your name, oh Mighty One, Omnipotent Creator, Holy Majesty of Creation, Benevolent Ruler and All-Merciful One." Ahtel bowed, feeling the Light of the Mighty One rushing through his very innermost being. "There are so many gathered, the sky has grown dark. Are there none to help me disperse them and bind them for the everlasting fire?"

"All things in my time, Warrior. Even as we speak, Ballelulia and Raphael are on their way along with Yoballa. Santero does not even suspect we will be there and has not bothered to show up himself. Beware lest these fallen are victorious. They have the potential for much sadness and grief on the planet Earth."

* * * * *

Wedge slept fretfully. Santero was sure to leave several of the fallen to guard him while he was away taking care of his other business. Wedge didn't know why he never seemed to wake up. It was as if he was living in a thick, thick fog and couldn't fight his way through it. It bothered him beyond measure and he struggled to wake up. It was like clawing his way back through a jungle of vines all gripping and pulling him down. He threw his head violently side to side. He saw a glimpse of Mia blending with faces out of a horror movie. It didn't make the remotest bit of sense to him. Finally he was able to wake up and see where he was: in Mia's bed overlooking the Pacific Ocean. He didn't even remember driving there. He looked at the moonlight reflecting on the waves and saw the early morning light ascending from the east. He wondered what he was doing in Mia's house and where she was. He took a step to the door and found himself being thrown back. He landed on his back and knocked his head. He attempted to get up and felt a heavy, dark presence holding him down. It was too much for him. He attempted to cry out and couldn't get out a word. He threw himself to the side and managed to get up.

He was in a panic. Something was after him from another world. He didn't know who or what they were or, for that matter, what they even wanted from him. A larger presence engulfed the room as Santero returned, enraged that Wedge had woken up. He realized reentering his body was not going to be as easy as before. Santero vaporized and attempted to enter Wedge through his nostrils. Wedge held his nostrils between his fingers and shook his head violently back and forth. The other fallen had gripped him around the legs and were making it impossible for him to continue his resistance. Wedge managed to pull his legs free and began to run through the master suite, toppling over chairs and side tables. He grabbed a large leather wing-back and threw it in front of him, shattering the large plate-glass window that overlooked the ocean. He made a dive and found himself in mid-air before he realized what he had done.

It didn't matter to him that he was going to die. He just wanted to be as far away as possible from the things that were pursuing him. The rocks opened their arms to him and granted him an almost instant death as his skull was crushed before his body toppled head first into the murky waters of the pre-dawn Pacific.

From the depth of the ocean he was amazed to find that he was swimming. He marveled at how he needed no oxygen, even underwater, and he began to dive deeper and deeper, exploring the treasures of the bay. Several shadows began to appear. He noticed them, but remained in awe of the intense peace he felt being set free from his human shell. The constrictions of the muscles, skin, and physical needs were all removed. He wondered if he had died and gone to Nirvana. Something gripped at his foot. He turned to look at a lizard-like creature with huge hooked hands that were impeding his swimming. Another creature that resembled an overgrown cyclops joined in and gripped him about the waist. Wedge struggled to no avail. They took him out to sea where they dragged him far below the surface. It was an endless pit of darkness and Wedge was no longer able to see anything around him. He was aware of a heat and saw black smoke. He began to detect the smell of sulfur. It was repugnant to him. He was chained and left in a pit. He was unable to move, even a little bit. He knew he hadn't gone to Heaven; he just hoped he hadn't gone to Hell.

Losing his human host made Santero more furious than he had been in a long, long time. He cursed the Mighty One for limiting his ability to appear in the physical realm. He was only allowed to change into a serpent and he knew even as crazy as people were in L.A., no one would buy talking to a serpent. Besides, he thought crawling around on one's belly would just get you flattened by a passing truck.

The Gods of War had managed to cloak their activities in secrecy and he had no idea that they were planning on destroying the entire shipment of Imps.

In a way, he was glad to be out of the human body with all of its limitations. He decided to return to the Circle of Light and taunt the Mighty One with his successes.

* * * * *

The Circle of Light glowed around the darkened form of Santero. No one spoke to him, but moved aside allowing him access to the Mighty One. The throngs in front of the Mighty One were enveloped in Praise and Worship and wondered how Santero could have ever forsaken his place as their worship leader and traded it for the kingdom of outer darkness. In the period of time that Santero had been separated from the Mighty One, the outer darkness had absorbed all the light that had permeated him from the eons he had worshipped the Mighty One. He no longer returned to pay homage or adoration to the very One who created him. He returned to challenge Him concerning His ability to lead and to assure himself of the Mighty One's non-interference in his planned destruction.

"You return, Santero. Have you seen how faithful my servant, Brian, has been? Surely you were wrong about My protection. He is quite willing on his own to follow me and walk according to My will, not his own."

"Yes, I see that, Mighty One," Santero spoke derogatively. "You promised not to interfere with my Imps. I am here to make sure that You will keep Your promise."

"I hear those who call unto me, Santero, and I answer them. I never leave them in situations too great for them. If My servants who are called by My name humble themselves and seek My face, then I will hear them and deliver them. I have not called them to face the sword but to experience My love."

"Keep them away from the Imps. The children of men are fascinated by the violence I weave into their daily lives. They are fascinated by the bloodshed and horror. I bring them only what they want."

"No, Santero," the Mighty One corrected, "you bring them what you have created an appetite for—their debasement. Because of the violence, they have learned to live with and accept as commonplace, you bring My creatures a sense of futility. You seek to kill that sensitivity which I placed in all of them. You seek to erase My nature from them and replace it with yours."

Santero rose as if to smite the Mighty One. "It is my nature they desire more than Yours, Mighty One. It is I and I alone who grants them their lusts. You tell them to walk a narrow road and caution them against life itself."

"No, you are so wrong. It is a life of love I call them to. I call them away from those things that harm them and others. My warriors will intervene and respond to My command, for it is I and not you that hold the very filaments of this universe together. I created you an eternal being, but lo, I wish I was able to remove you from my very memory, for it is indeed tragic that you shall live forever in your deception and the pain it will bring you. You say you like the fire, you say you thrive on the hate, but I know your true nature, Santero; you who were My favorite one, whose love I enjoyed, have disappointed Me more than all the others. Go, for there is no regret or sadness permitted here in my Circle of Light. Harm not My servant, and if the forces you bring upon him are beyond his means, he need only cry to Me and I will deliver him. Yes, though a thousand fall at his side, I will be with him always."

Santero departed. He knew he would need human hands to battle for his Imps.

* * * * *

Leslie Bailey was sound asleep on Terminal Island, an exclusive enclave in Long Beach. She was staying in a house belonging to her grandfather, who had made a fortune selling electronics to the Japanese in the 1950s. She had never been happy with her rather boring Presbyterian upbringing and had decided to delve into spiritism. At first it was relatively harmless, or so she thought. She read her astrology chart and consulted with palm readers every time she went to a renaissance festival or swap meet. She grew fascinated with it and began checking out books on all the dark arts. She turned her grandfather's old office into a seance room and had a pentagram painted on the hardwood flooring. Her bored friends would come over for her seances which more often than not would just be excuses to have sex with total strangers in the quest of spiritual enlightenment.

They had gathered at midnight as Leslie offered up her prayers from the Satanic Bible. She became acutely aware that something was different. She sat in the lotus position in the candlelit room and was both amazed and terrified that she would really get to contact someone from the dark side. Santero entered the room, furious that he had lost Wedge and reluctant, at first, to have to settle for Leslie. He floated about and vaporized into her nostrils which made her choke. She opened her mouth to speak and found herself unable to do so. She blacked out as he moved in to control her entire body. The rest of the group was too heavily drugged to pick up on the full implications on what had just happened. Santero left with his new body to head for the container to make sure it was unloaded and transferred safely.

Leslie had a new 28-foot Searay parked at her dock. It was difficult getting the boat keys out and steering the boat into the channel. It always took Santero a while to master the motor functions of anyone he possessed. It was tougher with this girl because she was quite a bit shorter than he was used to and quite intoxicated, so her responses resembled a severe case of palsy. If anyone would have looked at them controlling the craft, they would have known something was seriously wrong.

They passed several tugboat men who wolf-whistled at Leslie. Santero happily had Leslie flip them off. He relied on his feeling to guide him to the large container of Imps which had already been unloaded from the container boat by a crane and set on the ground waiting to be cleared by their customs broker.

Alice stopped at the pay phone at the end of the airline terminal and called Brian on his car phone as he was circling around the baggage claim areas at the huge L.A. airport. Traffic was just beginning to thicken but he found himself only minutes from her terminal. She set the phone down and turned to Bruce.

"He's in the Stealth," Alice stated. "It doesn't have much room. Should we just rent a car?"

"No, indeed not," Bruce stated. "I really feel that we need to get there now. If we miss this now, it'll be like trying to gather the feathers back from a down pillow that's blown all over creation."

Brian had already discovered the quickest route back and forth to Long Beach Harbor. When he pulled up in the Stealth, he had never been so happy to see Alice. One look at her face and he was reminded just how much he really treasured her and how lucky he was to have her as a wife and soul-mate.

"Hi, Brian," Bruce said as he extended his hand and climbed into the small seat in back. "I feel in my spirit we have no time to waste. Have you already been at the harbor?"

Brian was still hugging Alice when he looked up. "Yeah, I ran the numbers by Louie and left him down there. I can communicate to him with my cellular. Those container ships have lots of containers. I just hope Louie doesn't get run over looking for the right numbers. Hop in. Let's fly. It's going to take us a little more time now. Traffic is starting to congest."

They took the back road down the coast highway past San Pedro and Palos Verde. Brian flipped on his disc player and dialed in a Highest Praise CD. They all sang along, allowing themselves to be filled with the presence of the

Mighty One. Their guardians started to beam and grow stronger.

"This may not be so difficult after all, Yoballa," Ballelulia spoke.

"Indeed, all contact with the fallen is difficult. It leaves a sadness that only the waters of the Circle of Light are able to erase."

"I will leave and go ahead," Raphael spoke. "Ahtel is still over this city. Perhaps he and Gothos are on the situation now."

* * * * *

Raphael was at the harbor nearly instantaneously, just in time to notice the ambulance leaving with Louie Columbo. He saw the fallen dragging away the reluctant spirit and felt a certain dread on his behalf. He spotted the open container door and his ears turned towards the cacophony of voices. He had never heard so many spirits gathered at one time. Even the legion that the Mighty One's son had cast out were not this numerous. As he watched, he felt a presence come alongside him. He looked up and, nearly towering over him, was the beautiful face of Gothos. His hair was yellow white and he stood nearly eight feet tall. His chin was sharp and chiseled, and his eyes were the deepest blue. His hands were as large as Raphael had seen in the entire host of heavenly warriors, and Raphael knew that Gothos excelled as a champion and was unfearing in battle and extremely devoted to the Mighty One.

"Warrior Gothos," Raphael said, pleasantly surprised, "I am glad to see you are already here. Where is Ahtel?"

"He went to the Circle to request help from the Mighty One. They are everywhere and even their Lord Santero has arisen. These things must be very important to their plans," Gothos added.

"Yes, if we are unable to stop these, many people's lives will be destroyed. Do they know you are here?" Raphael whispered.

"I know Sawtooth suspects my presence. He has tasted my metal in past battles but I have remained cloaked. They just murdered someone who was attempting to hijack some of their shipment. There is the most unusual creature rolling about. It is a lobster but seems to be operating electronically. It is down there in the shadows across from the container."

"It belongs to one of the Mighty One's followers. Its name is Louie. It was left to monitor for them."

As they were speaking, Ahtel materialized next to them. "Greeting, praise be to the highest. The Mighty One informed me you were coming. Are any with you?"

"Yes, Yoballa and Ballelulia. He is still new to our warfare but has proven to be a most apt disciple to the craft." Raphael looked about. "Have you a plan?"

"I don't wish for direct contact with Santero. I trailed him back from the Circle of Light and saw him enter another human. He is now on his way over here in her boat. If you could prevent him from getting here, we could make sure that they are unable to unload this container. Praise be unto the highest." Raphael locked arms with Ahtel in a gesture of solidarity.

Raphael saw the small craft attempting to dock near the pier. He disappeared under the water and threw a piece of discarded chain into the propellers. Leslie lost all power to the craft and then began to drift away from the dock into the path of an oncoming tug towing a huge vessel behind it. The tug was unable to steer out of the way and rammed into the smaller craft splintering the hull and throwing Leslie overboard with the force of the impact. Captain Dan Sweeney looked and saw Leslie go into the bay and cursed her for being where she shouldn't have, making him have the first accident of his nearly unmarred command. He pulled his horn "AHOOGA" and called to his first mate.

"Lifeboat starboard side!" Sweeney instinctively cut his powerful engine hoping she wouldn't get swept up in them and be torn to shreds. The sheer momentum of their power pushed them past the wreckage and down channel after quarter mile.

Frank Henderson lowered the lifeboat and started the small outboard motor. The Searay was heavily listing having taken a direct hit to the front port side. Only the rear of the craft was still above water. Frank looked for the person who had gone overboard and was shocked when a hand grasped on to the side of his lifeboat.

He cut his engine and stood up to grab the survivor. He was surprised to see it was a small woman with very blonde hair who couldn't have weighed more than a hundred pounds. In normal circumstances, he would have found her very attractive, but she was covered with channel sludge and mumbling incoherently.

Santero debated on whether to wait it out inside Leslie or try to find another host. He decided to wait it out, hoping the accident wouldn't impede him. Frank threw a blanket over the woman and headed back to the tug. The Coast Guard and Harbor Police had been notified immediately, and the harbor skiff was already pulling up to the tug as they approached.

Over the megaphone the Harbor Police called out, "Any other survivors?"

Frank stood tying the small lifeboat back to the overhanging cables. "No, she was the only one aboard."

"Roger, we'll get an ambulance. Raise her up and we'll transfer her into the craft."

Santero was beginning to grow furious. If he attempted to bolt, he knew everyone in the harbor would be looking for his host. If he waited, he was wasting valuable time. He prompted Leslie to wake. She stood up shaking off the water and trying to straighten her hair, still very much inebriated.

"It's okay. Really, I don't need any medical attention," she slurred.

"If I were you, miss, I wouldn't say anything." Frank had her sit back down. "They'll throw you in jail for operating under the influence here. It would be best if you just lay back and let them take you to the hospital. If you're lucky, they won't run any alcohol tests on you and all you'll lose is your boat—not your freedom."

The Harbor Police pulled up alongside the lifeboat. A paramedic supervised the loading of Leslie's body. While Santero was still debating what to do, the paramedic began praying over the body. He looked at the tatoo of the pentagram placed between her breasts and called out to the Mighty One.

"Oh God, I bind every power from hell that would seek to take this child from Your mercies, Your loving kindness. I call on You in the name of Your only begotten Son, whatsoever I bind on earth is bound in heaven."

Santero hated prayer. He did his best to stay away from it at all times. He decided to leave the body and fight in the unseen dimension. As he tried to leave, he found his passageway blocked. He couldn't believe that the prayer of an idiot had bound him in the incapacitated body. He thrashed about, causing the police to react and bind Leslie's body onto the stretcher with restraints.

Leslie became aware of the presence within her and also became aware of her pain. "Help," she cried in a muffled voice, "I can't breathe. I'm burning up."

The Harbor Police had radioed an air emergency helicopter to take her to the UCLA Trauma Center, about 15 minutes away. Her body was loaded by the Air-Vac team as she continued to cry out that she was burning up. They rolled her down the hallway into the emergency room where they stripped off her clothing and began a thorough exam for physical trauma. They did a full body x-ray and a CAT scan looking for signs of brain hemorrhage. Two of the x-ray techs were from Seoul, Korea where they attended the church of Paul Yonggi Cho. They knew what the Pentagram on her chest represented and they joined hands and prayed for her even as they waited for the x-rays.

She sat straight up and looked at them. "Where am I?" she asked.

"You've been in an accident." The young doctor motioned her to lie back down.

She sat up again and said in a deep voice, "Let me off this table, you miserable excuse for a human being, before I tear your head from your neck."

Leslie reached over to strike out at the young doctor closest to her. He jumped back and looked at her in shock.

"Don't pray for her any longer," Santero roared. "This girl is mine, all mine."

The two doctors joined hands and each laid them on her shoulders pushing her back on the gurney.

"No, I'm afraid not. Whatever we touch, wherever we walk, whatever we speak, agreeing together is the Lord's, the Mighty One. Shut up, foul spirit. Do not speak. Do not harm this girl."

"I am the wrath of darkness. What do you know of power and authority? You serve a crucified God who died in weakness and suffering. I am the triumphant one."

The two doctors stepped aside as Leslie's body laid back down. They discussed her case.

"We'd best phone for help. This is a very serious case. This girl has opened herself up to total possession. This kind will not come up except with much prayer and fasting."

They gave her a shot of heavy barbiturates to keep her under and wheeled her down the hall where they put her in a straightjacket and tied her into a bed. As the orderlies were tying her down, they went to the phone and called their local church prayer chain and started a massive landslide which buried Santero even further.

CHAPTER SIXTEEN

SITTING BY THE DOCK

Brian maneuvered his Stealth close to the fence that was meant to keep outsiders from the dock area.

"Louie is positioned down there. Let me get him and see if he's got a reading on the container numbers."

"What are we going to do when we have the numbers? How are you going to stop them from getting through?" Alice questioned.

"To begin with," Bruce stepped forward," we need to ask the Mighty One for His help if there's a hundred thousand of those Imps in those containers. Someone from the fallen is going to be here making sure they get through."

As he spoke, the ambulance went by.

"Something is going on down here already. Let's pray."

The group bowed their heads, closed their eyes, and joined hands together. They felt as if they were lifted off the ground. Their heads grew light and a current of energy seemed to join them as if there was an electrical charge flowing unrestricted through each of them. Bruce cried out in a language only known to the Mighty One and His warriors. Yoballa, Ballelulia, and Ahtel were standing nearby and began to receive a supercharge of power as the current formed a triangulated pattern, reflecting off the Mighty One eons away in the Circle of Light. It was beamed back to them with a thousand times more power. The prayer was short but effective. As they opened their eyes, Brian knew the Mighty One had planted the solution in his heart. He dialed his cellular and contacted Louie, who was equipped for short-distance, two-way communication.

"Louie, come in. Have you found the containers?" Brian held the phone close to his ear.

"Have visual sight of number Frt. 98874, container Frt. 98875 being unloaded by crane now."

"Louie, where are they?"

"Pier W-1, very end."

Brian hung up the phone. "Alright, we've got to get to pier W-1. Bruce, help me with my frequency jamming device." Brian hit the lock to his trunk. It swung open automatically. "It's in there. Alice, go down and see if there are any workers down by pier W-1."

"What if there are?"

"Tell them anything. Get them away from the crane. If this frequency jammer doesn't work, I'm going to have to dump both containers in the bay."

"You can't," Alice protested. "They'll arrest you."

"Maybe so, maybe not. Look, I'm taking responsibility for what I've made. It's my fault. I've got to do what I think is right. I've got to undo what I've done before anybody else dies."

Bruce, holding the portable generator, walked over. "Alice, he's right. If these things aren't stopped now, who knows if we'll even have a country left!"

Yoballa went forward with Bruce, keeping an eye out for the fallen. As they rounded the fence and they walked down between rows of empty containers being shipped back to Hong Kong and Singapore, Yoballa saw Sawtooth. Sawtooth had a crazed look on his face and challenged him.

"Go no further, Warrior Yoballa." Sawtooth sharpened his talons. "I have been given charge to protect this shipment."

"Step aside, Sawtooth." Yoballa stood proudly, being joined by Raphael and Gothos. "We are many today."

Maduke, Matush, and Cadaver flanked the warriors. Cadaver stepped forward. "Your charge must die."

The fallen flew to the top of the stack of empty containers. Brian was trailing Bruce by a few paces and looked up when he heard a creaking. He saw the container on top begin to topple directly over Bruce. Brian threw his transmitter to the ground, dove and pushed Bruce away from the falling containers.

"Your cheap tricks of moving objects bore me," Raphael spoke, winding his arm in a circle as his light band stretched out further and further like a giant lariat. As Cadaver flew down to challenge him, Raphael released the light band catching Cadaver about the neck.

"Cursed," Cadaver grimaced in pain. "This burns. Get it off me." Cadaver looked at his cohorts. "Don't stand there; cut the band."

Maduke cautiously flew forward, his sabre drawn, trying to cut the light band to release Cadaver. Before he could cut it, his thrust was parried by Yoballa, and they battled hand-to-hand. His thrust was parried and feathers flew as they tumbled through the air. Matush flew up with his barbed spear and jabbed it into Yoballa's back, wounding him just as he was about to get the upper hand over Maduke. Before Matush could impale him, he found himself being swung into the air by Ahtel.

Gothos threw his light band around Cadaver, further binding him and rendering him unable to even lift his sword. Ahtel took to the air to bind Matush who saw him coming and attempted to escape. He made it over the bay where Ahtel dove, bringing him down as easily as a falcon would bring down a crow.

Ahtel dragged him over and bound him to a buoy.

"I'll dispose of you later, Matush." Ahtel looked at him with fury. "I never knew you to run from a battle before. Your age has cowered you."

Ahtel had faced Matush in a deadly battle over the body of Moses thousands of years before and had known him as a brutal enemy. To see him flee in battle trying to save his own leathery skin, filled him with pity. He flew back to guard Bruce and Brian from further attack.

The battle raged around them though they were quite unaware. Bruce picked himself up and stared in disbelief at the containers. He retrieved the generator which laid in shambles.

"Brian, I'm afraid there's no salvaging this. It's trashed. What are we going to do now?"

"Plan B," Brian smiled. "Never paint yourself in a corner, unless you use quick-drying paint. I've got no choice but to dump the containers. Hopefully the pier is empty. They should be going through a shift change; I checked earlier. New shift comes on at 8."

Bruce looked at his watch. "They're going to throw the book at all of us. We can't just go destroying other people's property."

"You're right," Brian spoke. "I knew we can't, but in this case, it's the only alternative. Without that generator, I can't deprogram these things. You want a bunch of these little Imps rolling around?"

They ran down the pier trying to spot Alice. When they found her, she was looking through the binoculars at the crane hooked up to the container 98874.

"Brian, the second container is still on the ship. I watched the man get out of the crane with his lunch box. It doesn't look like he's coming back."

"Where's Louie?" Brian asked.

"Right here," Louie said, rolling out. "Maintaining visual contact."

"Look, Alice, what I am going to do could pretty well mess up our entire lives but there's no other choice. The containers that fell over just about killed us and destroyed the generator. I can't deprogram these things. They've got to be destroyed. Wait here. If anybody comes, call Louie on the cellular. I'll have him with me."

Brian picked up Louie.

"Where are we going?" Louie asked.

"Don't worry about that," Brian answered. "Just keep a lookout for anyone coming."

"Bruce, after I dump the one, you are going to have to hook up the cables to that one over there."

It was fortunate that the container ship was the only ship on the pier. As Brian climbed into the crane, he noticed that the key was left in it. He studied the controls and pushed the lever right in front of him. He watched as the container rocked back and forth. He reached for the control lever on his right and pulled it to the left. The container rose above the ship and started moving on the giant cable over the pier. He decided it would be best to dump it in the harbor on the other side. He studied the controls to see how the cable detached. Fortunately, it was on an electromagnetic switch and wouldn't have to be manually released. Otherwise, he would have to go into the water and release it. While Bruce and Alice watched, he swung the giant steel container, which looked more like a semi-box over their head, and dropped it in the cold waters of the harbor. He smiled and pushed the control lever back over and swung the cable over the container sitting on the pier. Bruce climbed up the container, keeping clear of the swinging cable which hooked in four places. He secured the first two and looked over at Alice, who was talking to a security guard.

"Get down off of there," the guard stated. "I don't know who you think you are, but in a minute you'll be talking to the police."

"Okay," Bruce stated, "I just have to get this other cable hooked up. I'll be right down. Just helping my friend out."

Bruce hooked up the other side of the cable and climbed down off the container. He approached the guard. As he was approaching the guard, the container began to rise and distracted the guard's attention. Bruce grabbed Alice and motioned her to run. They started running off the pier. The guard unholstered his gun and fired in the air. They never looked back and turned between a group of stacked containers.

The guard watched with a bewildered look as Brian swung the container over the harbor and released it into the bay. He got on his walkie talkie and called for backup. Brian got out of the crane and climbed down carrying Louie. He walked down the pier to the waiting harbor police whose guns were drawn and pointed dead at him.

"Hands in the air!" the loudspeaker called out.

Brian lifted his hands holding Louie in them.

"I am not carrying a gun," Brian shouted. "It's just a pet."

Three officers rushed up to him, took Louie out of his hands, and cuffed him. They forced him into the back of the squad jeep.

Cadaver watched in horror as the second container was dropped into the water. He knew that the Imps would be destroyed and the "Small Ones" would just stay underwater, but he wished he could escape his light bands and lead them away—anywhere.

"It's too late, Cadaver," Raphael said, leading him away. "Evil will never truly triumph over good. For all of your planning, look what you have wrought. Santero has no authority except the fear he rules by."

Sawtooth watched from the distance as many of the fallen were led away. He wondered why Santero had not come and personally supervised the safe arrival of the small ones. It didn't matter anymore. He knew there would always be those who would foolishly buy their evil schemes. He knew evil would always live in the hearts of men, and their lives would always be easy prey.

Alice and Bruce left the shipyards. Alice knew it was senseless for them to be arrested too. "After all," she reasoned, "someone would have to put up his bail and pay for damages." For once she was truly happy that Brian was only seventeen. She knew at the most he would probably get a slap on the wrist and a few months in a juvenile facility—or maybe just supervisory probation.

Bruce watched her looking at Brian being put in the squad car. "Let's go. We did all we could. The rest is in His hands."

THE END

EPILOGUE

Alice hired the most expensive defense attorney in Los Angeles who, after six months of motions and countermotions, managed to get Brian's case heard in juvenile court. Damages were paid to Tannersly for the full value of the shipment and charges were reduced to trespassing. Brian was let off with one year of supervised probation.

Mia Tannersly scrapped all plans to market the "IMPS" and went back to Hong Kong where she sold her interests in Tannersly Industries and went into missionary work supplying food and Christian literature to the underground church in Communist China.

The containers with the Imps were dredged up and stored in a warehouse in Compton, California where they were forgotten.

The City of Los Angeles was spared from the curse of the "Imps," but still faced the daily problems caused by the callousness and sin of its inhabitants.

Brian Phillips went back to Stanford and worked on projects in the robotic field designing body parts for those who were missing them from birth defects and accidents. He became interested in medicine and used his wealth to find ways to give mobility back to people with permanent spinal injuries.

Leslie Bailey awoke in the hospital feeling confused and bewildered, yet remarkably at peace. Santero's spirit was cast out of her and she made her peace with the Mighty One. She went to a skin specialist and had her pentagram tatoo removed. She used her time and energy to speak with young people throughout the United States of the danger of dabbling with fortune tellers, palm readers, tarot cards, astrology, ouija boards, and seances. She ended up marrying a Christian evangelist and traveled to Africa with him where they preached at crusades.